Polaris Special:
Dui's True Ending

Book 3.5 of the Series

Dui
对

ISBN-13: 978-0-9966338-3-3

Other Titles in the Series:
Polaris: Emperor of Nan Rong
Polaris: Empress of Ning
Polaris: The Demon General and the General Practitioner

Polaris Special: Dui's True Ending

By Lenne Penry

Polaris Special: Dui's True Ending

Chapter 1: The General Practitioner

Nearly six months have passed since the conflict between Bei Ling and Nan Rong. For the most part, life in the Southland has resumed a steady pace and with time, so has disquiet from the sorrowful memories of those days gone by. The topic of war has grown mundane. Food and fashion are all the rage and with spring peeking its head through the little buds beginning to sprout on the surrounding peach trees, so is love. Love and marriage to be exact. There hasn't been a day since late February when the clinic has gone without chatter of upcoming engagement parties and the Spring Lovers' Festival over in Lu Xu Village.

There is an old tradition, usually reserved for girls from wealthier families, to stand from a tall balcony and toss down a red silk ball to a crowd of interested men. The man to catch said ball, would become her betrothed. The festival in Lu Xu is supposedly similar, except there isn't the same commitment. It's merely for amusement and all girls are allowed to participate, regardless of their fortune. Well, that's what I heard, anyhow. I've never actually been to Lu Xu. Aside from the fact that I was too much of a tomboy most of my life, Master Tai Hung never would have permitted such frivolity.

Being back here again, in Pa Xu, is achingly nostalgic. Practically every inch of this village reminds me of the master, which makes me realize I was lucky to have had as many years with him as I did, despite my insolence. He was my family. I'm glad that after everything, even without Master Tai Hung, I have found a place to call home.

The little bell on the door of the clinic jingles. In walks another nostalgia-inducing face. His hair is a bit messier than usual and the slight frown on his mouth has become so common that I know exactly what he'll say.

"I can't believe Guan raised the price on wormwood again!"

Having the words taken out of his mouth, Dui's half-parted lips swiftly become a pout. His eyes roll and then the physician drops the satchel onto the floor.

"He's doing it out of spite. I just know it!"

"There are other trade shops. You don't have to keep going back there."

"If it weren't for the quality, I wouldn't."

He says that, but I know it's really because of Master Tai Hung. Twenty years ago, my master was his mentor, back when Guan's grandfather ran the Magnolia Trade Shop. Often, Dui and I accompanied Master Tai Hung during his trek in from Tian Mao Yi Temple to purchase medicinal herbs and supplies. Dui continues to visit the same shop out of habit, despite his irritation for Guan, and maybe also out of nostalgia.

"Want me to go next time? Guan usually gives me a discount. I think you must have slighted him."

"Hmph! As if I even have free time to go around slighting buffoons! He's just jealous and spiteful." The physician settles onto the floor and goes through the parcel of ingredients.

Same old, same old. He's always griping about the jealous and spiteful Guan and yet refuses to provide reasons for his conclusions.

It's late afternoon. We only had six patients today. That seems to be about the most we can expect. Unlike the crowded capital, work here is laid back, and as Dui has taken on two other apprentices from Tian Mao Yi Temple, the village will soon have more physicians than it needs, which to Dui, is a good thing. More knowledgeable people will be able to find more cures, that's his belief. Ending earthly suffering is his ambition.

"Next time the buffoon comes over for treatment, I'll demand payment through a wagon of wormwood."

"Wow, Dui. You're much crankier than usual. Maybe this will cheer you up. A hoard of girls came over while you were out and demanded to know whether the *handsome* doctor will attend the festival in Lu Xu. You're becoming very popular with the ladies."

"They're just nosy and you're imagining things."

"Nuh-uh. Almost every other young woman has asked me about your situation."

"Like I said, nosy."

"They're interested, Dui. I said I didn't know just because well, I really don't know which of the misses you might consider. What should I tell them?"

A tinge of discomfiture breaks across half-knitted brows. He momentarily shuffles before letting out a soft sigh. "I'm not the only popular one. Men have been asking about you, especially Guan. I told you he was jealous. You know my stance. I think you should marry and start a family. You're not getting any younger. I'm worried about you."

"I know. And I'm worried about you."

"Well, don't. I'll manage. You shouldn't sacrifice happiness to keep me company."

"That's not what I meant. I'm worried you've gone deaf since I've told you for the hundredth time that I'm happy here."

"Then, you're insane. Think things over. This isn't best for you in the long run. The next time someone asks—"

"The next time someone asks about me, tell him I've already been smitten by another."

"That's a hard fib to keep when *that other* is in the capital. Every man will think I'm lying to keep you for myself."

"I didn't mean Bai Hu."

"No? Then who?"

The casual attitude is unexpected. I thought he would, was hoping he would, feel a bit more anxious. After all, my heart is beating so rapidly, I can't keep from rocking back and forth. There seems to be spiders crawling over my hands and arms, face and head; I'm scratching at a phantom itch. This keeps happening every time I think I've worked up the nerves and then I always default to the norm and end up kicking myself afterwards for being a coward.

Recently, I've teased him about other women, while truly, I've been secretly jealous of the attention he's garnered. Dui's grown more serious, reserved, and actually manlier than the unkempt, listless doctor I met in An. He hasn't felt the compulsion to behave lecherously toward any woman, though now, I wonder if any would deny his advances. He's become so mature and maybe, I feel a bit intimidated.

When his question goes unanswered, Dui sets the box of mullein onto the floor and looks up. I can feel my face burning brighter from having his attention; the pang in my chest is growing tight.

"Are you embarrassed, Bao Lai? Oh, I see. He and I may not get along but that's no reason to keep your distance. I'll tell the buffoon to come over next time I see him."

"Wh-What? I don't like Guan."

"Good, I don't either. So, out with it. Who is it?"

"Y...You?"

"What about me?"

He's shuffling the herbs again, completely ignoring me as though he couldn't care less my answer. I'd practice this exchange inside my mind a million times and this isn't even close to the romantic scene I'd hoped.

The phantom itch is becoming worse. At this rate, I'm going to scratch off all the skin on my arms. "I... uh... I like—love, I really... love um... Tsk! *Can you please stop fussing over the herbs and look up?!*"

That came out much louder and more irate than I intended. His shoulders stiffen and the Dui's posture slowly straightens.

"And you call me cranky. What is it?"

Grey eyes are now on me and my loose nerves are starting to slip away. During our time in Feng Jia, Dui confessed his love for me but at the time, emotional turmoil and engrossment over Bai Hu kept me from having seriously considered him. The truth is these rioting feelings in my chest for Dui aren't actually newfound. I realized some time ago that I loved him all along, maybe even before Feng Jia. It's unnerving and downright painful to have the person I love look at me this way, the same look he gives everyone else. I don't know why I'm still such a coward after everything we've been through.

"Who's a coward?"

Ugh, mouthing my thoughts again. I've been trying to keep that under control but some bad habits die hard.

"You—I mean me. I'm the coward, Dui. I shouldn't have waited this long to tell you."

"Tell me what?"

"That I... love... you? Ack! That wasn't supposed to be a question! Stop being such a coward! I love you! I love you! I love you, Dui! *Phew*! Boy, that felt *good* to get off my chest! Want to have lunch now?"

The itch disappeared and still, I'm a jittery mess. Surging blood makes me light headed; my cheeks just might explode. While I fumble about like an idiot, he's turned into a statue. The wide-eyed stare and pallid cheeks are inexplicably adorable. This is a reaction more appropriate than his former disinterest. I don't know what I was worried about. Dui loves me, of course, he said so himself.

Seconds turn to minutes. The awkward silence is terribly drawn out. He's not likely to get over the shock any time soon so I might as well help him along.

Leaning across the pile of supplies on the floor, my quivering lips approach his frozen mouth. However, before they could even brush, he's flown back toward the door.

"I-I forgot something important at th-the... trade shop! Late shipment should be coming in soon. Have a good night! Don't wait up!"

And he's out the door.

Chapter 2: A Confession Come Too Late

The little bell on the door jingles. He reaches up to silence the jovial greeting as a mean to steady his own nerves but the trinket has fulfilled its purpose. Slowly, I lift off the floor from behind the low table where our dinners are laid. The food's cold and so are Dui's fully flushed cheeks from the chilly night air. His hair is disheveled, his clothes are wrinkled, and in his hand is a small satchel.

"Mmh. It's so late. Are you just now coming in? You know how easily the cold air makes you sick, Dui. Come over and warm up."

He stares at the blanket over my body which I've stretched out in invitation. It's not unusual for us to be close. However, the moment his eyes widen is the same moment I realize the confession made can't be undone. We're not just friends anymore; I also don't know what we are.

"Were you waiting for me?" He inserts quietly while treading closer toward the backroom where supplies and medicines for the clinic are stored.

"Of course. We always have dinner together. I made your favorite."

"Thanks. I'm not hungry. Eat up and go to bed. I have to put some things away. Good night." The mechanical performance is that of a third-rate actor.

Dui dodges into the backroom and then closes the door behind.

I don't know what to make of this. Maybe it's conceited and egotistical, but of all the people in the world, I never imagined Dui would be the one to reject me. He said he loved me and I thought he always would. People may change but I can always count on Dui. He's been the single constancy in my life for the past year. More than anything, I'm afraid to lose his companionship.

"Dui. Let me put that away. You go wash up."

After sliding into the backroom, I manage to steal the satchel. There's nothing inside and nothing new he's placed on the shelf.

"What's going on? Did you walk around all night just to ignore me? Not just tonight but the entire afternoon too. Dui, you don't have to run from me. I'm your friend."

The doctor shuffles uncomfortably from his exposed fib. I know why he lied. I just wish he hadn't.

"I'm not ignoring you," he mumbles.

"Yes, you are. You won't even look at me. I know why you... if you don't love me, just say so. I'm not forcing you to accept me, Dui. Being with you, close to you, is enough for me. After everything we've been through, I just thought..."

"Thought that I... worshipped you?"

"Not in those exact terms, but yes. I know it's conceited."

"It is. That part doesn't surprise me. What is surprising is your timing. Why confess now? When did you even love me?"

"For a while. Maybe... before Feng Jia."

"So what's kept you?"

Those usual gentle eyes are hard and seemingly cold. He knows the answer and apparently that answer is also the cause for his distance. Bai Hu, my childhood friend, whom I'd fallen for in An, was the reason I couldn't accept Dui's confession prior. Hu was important to me and I loved him. Due to unusual circumstances, he relinquished our relationship. I ran after Dui to find a place to belong. I ran after Dui because Bai Hu rejected me.

My lowered head signals that I've realized his distress. He moves back two steps to farther our distance.

"Dui, I'm sorry. It wasn't right of me to overlook your pride—"

"Pride has nothing to do with it. For your own sake, don't mistake loneliness for attraction. Should Hu changes his mind, I know where I would belong."

"What are you saying? I'm not mistaken. I've loved you since An!"

"Then you should have said something when I was killing myself pining over you. I've given up the notion of love between us, in spite of my worship, and yes, I still worship you. I've placed you on a pedestal too high to ever reach. I've accepted defeat."

"Since when did the stubborn Dr. Dui become a quitter?"

"Once he realized a lost war is not worth fighting. Think about it, you would never willingly consider me without his rejection. There are other men—"

"I don't want other men! How can you say that I wouldn't love you without Hu's rejection when Hu isn't here and I love you all the same?"

"That's right. Hu isn't here, that's why you think you love me. I can't indulge your delusions, even if I'm not against them. Maybe I don't deserve much but I won't accept being loved by default."

It is a matter of pride. I know it. I've put Bai Hu before him too many times for Dui not to feel resentment. I felt the same when Hu put Kai before me. Had she rejected him and Hu came back to me, I would have been more enraged than happy for his previous dismissal. I'd just assumed Dui would always forgive my insults, would always *worship* me, as he'd said. I threw out a few words of love and expected his immediate devotion. This insult was one too many.

He moves away another step, and in response, I take a step back in concession. I may have assumed his affection but I understand his feelings. The farther I push him to accept me, the farther resentment will call for his withdrawal. What we had was comfortable and familiar and I greedily opened an old wound which never healed for a chance at something more. I love Dui, and yet I've not learned to put him first, the way he's always accomplished for me. All this time, I haven't become worthy of this selfless man.

"You deserve better than the best, Dui. I'm sorry. It was careless of me. I won't bring it up again."

Sometime after I've turned in for the night, the backroom door quietly opens and then the same footsteps I would recognize anywhere, shuffle quietly into the room adjacent.

Chapter 3: Messenger from An

Fifty percent off wormwood! Dui would be proud, at least, he would be if we were speaking much to one another. The day is fairly cool. I volunteered to run over for more wormwood during lunch to give the physician some time alone. Guan was more than accommodating. I never would have known that he favored me until Dui mentioned it.

Years ago when my master and I visited the Magnolia Trade Shop, Guan usually gave me a once over and then walked away, nose raised and shoulders squared. Maybe he still hasn't realized I was the pup who dawdled beside Master Tai Hung, but I guess I shouldn't be surprised considering my peculiarity then. Then, I was cross-dressed to fit in with the temple boys. In fact, I've cross-dressed most of my life until becoming the Demon General's pretense wife. Hu purchased for me this pink robe, which I still often wear. Through him, I finally accepted myself as a woman.

Hu's done much for me. When I look back at the circumstances which drove him into the arms of another, I can't feel angry, neither do I blame him. I loved Hu. Through my own carelessness, we were driven apart. I'm afraid of history repeating itself. I don't want to lose Dui. Dui's always been supportive, and despite my bad habit of tormenting him ever since our time at Tian Mao Yi, he's always forgiven me. This time, it's not that simple. Nowadays, whenever our eyes connect, they would again awkwardly diverge. I don't know what I can say to erase the burden I've placed over his heart. Even if I can take back my confession, I don't know if I would. I love Dui. He has been my friend, my family, and my beloved. The notion of being without him is inconceivable and yet, another notion is also true: I can't be content through mere friendship. I want more from Dui.

"Hi there!"

"Ack!"

The gentle hand landing on my shoulder quickly turns dream world upside down. He laughs nervously at the quick withdrawal, which nearly ended with my face slamming against the ground.

"Sorry! So jumpy, Miss Bao Lai! Long time no see!"

It's only been half a year and his voice has grown twice as deep. His youthful face still carries a hint of innocence but that's certainly a man standing there and not the boy I remember. Qing Hai, Hu's trainee and coined best tracker of the imperial army, was a good friend to both Dui and me during our time in An.

"What are you doing here, Qing Hai?"

"Ha-ha! Does that mean you're not happy to see me?"

"S-Sorry! I didn't mean it like that!"

"I know," he smiles kindly with an extended helping hand. "I was on my way over to the clinic when you wandered across my path with your head in the cloud. I didn't mean to scare you. How are you and Master Dui?"

"I'm fine. Dui's... fine, too. What about you? I almost didn't recognize you, Qing Hai. Did you get taller?"

"Glad you noticed. General Hu refuses to admit that I'm catching up to him. He's as stubborn as ever."

Despite his playful demeanor, I can't share Hai's amusement. The moment that name projects from his lips, a cold chill spreads across my chest.

"Qing Hai, h-how is Bai Hu?"

"Same old slave driver. I'm not his trainee anymore and he still bosses me around in the barracks. If only he didn't outrank me! Ah, well."

The same casual shrug befits the young soldier. He smiles as if oblivious to my anxiety.

"G-Good. I'm glad he's doing well."

Another question is on the tip of my tongue, one that is slightly inappropriate. How could I not be curious when it comes to the man who was once my entire world? I really shouldn't care if he's married to Kai or if he loves someone else altogether, and still, I do. Maybe Dui's implications weren't farfetched. Should Hu change his mind about me, I'm not sure how I would react. I love Dui but I can't deny the part of me which perpetually feels hopeful for Hu's attention.

"*Hello*, Miss Bao Lai! You're spacing out again!" Hai snickers in that familiar boyish manner. "Oh, right! I have a letter for you. It came from Ming Na so I figured it should be delivered personally considering... you know."

He draws a neatly folded letter from inside the chest plate. On the last line is the name of the sender. Now, that is surprising.

"It's getting late. I should be going, Miss Bao Lai."

"Wait, don't you want to see Dui?"

"I can't. Uncle wants a letter delivered to a nobleman the town over."

"Come back after your delivery and have dinner with us."

"Sorry. It's recruitment season and I was put in charge. Uncle permitted three days and it's taken over a day and a half to reach Pa Xu. I have to start out before sundown. Maybe next time, hmm?"

It took six months for us to have this five-minute reunion. How many years will it take for a full day?

"Don't look so disappointed! I'll come back in the fall, Miss Bao Lai! I promise. Sometime around the Harvest Festival."

"Y-Yes. You're right. Spring is a busy season in the capital. The Mid-Autumn Harvest Festival will be a good time. I'll see you then. Stay safe."

"The war's over, Miss Bao Lai, but thanks, I will."

He smiles courteously and then with a swift bow, makes for Pa Xu's stables.

The war's over he said, and yet this letter in my hand brings an ominous feeling that another is on the verge of beginning.

Chapter 4: Journey North

Oh, goodness. I wasn't expecting this. One step inside the clinic and the hoard of admirers encircling Dui are ready to tear me apart with their vicious stares. His dream of being surrounded by multiple women at once has come true; and yet, the physician couldn't be more uncomfortable. Grey eyes dart furiously back and forth before setting on the satchel in my hand.

"Is that the wormwood? Good. We have orders to fill. If you'll please excuse me, ladies."

Dui stumbles away for dear life, clumsily grabs the satchel, and then makes haste into the backroom. His admirers are seething though I can't imagine their huffy expressions are different from my own. I've nothing nice to say, hence, I follow the doctor.

Once the backroom door closes, an irate flush of fury fills the adjacent room during the women's retreat, ending with a heavy slam of the wooden front door against the frame. At Dui's old clinic in the capital, women often left in the same manner, except their irritation was stemmed from Dui's lecherous groping. Nowadays, always from his disregard. While he once flirted with every woman who crossed his path, Dui couldn't find pleasure in their companies. For some reason or other, I was the first woman to whom he'd grown attached. I had hoped that I would also be the last.

25

"Hey, Dui."

"Hmm?"

A few months ago, he would have looked up and smiled whenever I called to him. Recently, even before our squabble, he hasn't been as attentive. I hadn't realized before now that most days when we sit together, he usually looks to the floor or out the window, seemingly joyless. The attachment between us must have grown mundane. He said that he still worships me, maybe that too was out of good humor. If nothing else, his detachment will make this parting much simpler.

"I, um... I need to take some time off."

"Take as long as you need. I doubt we'll have another patient for the rest of the day."

"That's not what I meant. The thing is, I ran into Qing Hai earlier."

"Oh? Where is he?"

"He left, actually, being the busy soldier that he is. Anyway, Hai delivered this letter and um... some old friends need help. I... I have to leave for a while. Probably for at least a month or so. Will you be all right alone or should I run over to Tian Mao Yi and send for Gai and Wan?"

Considering the discomfiture wreaking havoc on his nerves these past several days, the news should have brought a sigh of relief. Instead, the frozen doctor slowly swings his stiff body away from the storage shelf. A heavy frown settles over his mouth.

"Where are you going?"

"Ming Na."

"The E Mo city?"

"You know them? And yes. Something's happened and they want my help."

"The E Mo don't care for outsiders. I was only permitted entry to provide treatment for a young girl when their elders couldn't. How do you know them?"

"Remember when I said that during the conflict I was held captive in Ji You? I was taken in because Captain Xian dressed me one of the E Mo hostages. I was with them for a time."

The E Mo are a tribal group to the north, sometimes called barbarians due to their severance from society in favor of seclusion in the desert on the outskirts of Xia Pa. During the Nan Rong – Bei Ling conflict, E Mo women and children were held captive in Ji You to force the men's compliance. Horrible exploitations and mistreatments befell the captives, including sexual abuse and physical assault by Bei Ling's soldiers. Just the thought of it still makes me sick to my stomach.

Through Captain Xian's albeit asinine plan, the captives were freed. I made two new friends and came to terms with the Demon Slayer blood in my veins. My gift, passed down from the great warrior Fa Zhen, allows me to seemingly stop time. Though the letter doesn't say, I believe this is the same reason why my presence was requested.

"I'm coming with you."

"Wh-huh? Y-You can't, Dui."

"Am I still too much of a burden for you?"

"Of course not! What about your patients?"

"Which patient? One person came today for a mild runny nose. Yesterday had two suffering from mere coughs. Gai and Wan can handle that much."

"But..."

The last time Dui ran after me to Feng Jia, he nearly died. Rushing toward danger just makes him jump headfirst to keep me safe. In all probability, this trip won't be without danger.

"I can take care of myself, Bao Lai. You don't have to worry."

"I'm not. I just find it odd. Sure you want to come? There won't be any chance of avoiding me, the way you've going about. I'll cuddle up to you on cold nights, might even try to hold your hands, and make you talk to me the entire way."

"I thought you weren't going to bring that up again."

The tone is hard. A corner of his mouth twitches from displeasure. Those eyes are without one fleck of sentiment. He's looking at me in the same manner he had to those women: completely apathetic. At this rate, it makes no sense for him to even come. He wants to protect me out of sheer duty, unlike previously, out of love. Duty is not enough of a reason to risk his safety. Love is my reason for keeping him from harm.

Still, I know him too well. No matter what I say, he's still as stubborn as a mule. I might as well concede.

"Sorry. You're right. I'll send for Gai and Wan. Why don't you start packing?"

Chapter 4 – 2

In contrast to a year ago, I've learned to do many things, such as ride a horse and utilize simple navigation techniques. Dui taught these skills to me, along with many others, so that I've become more adept. Dui's always full of useful knowledge. Somewhere along the way, I've taught him a few of my not-so-useful ones.

It's been a week since I left the clinic and pretended to call for Dui's apprentices from the temple. I actually rented a horse from the stable and started north. The E Mo wouldn't have sent for an outsider unless the situation is dire. Inside of the distant person he's become is a man who won't stop running after me. Dui's grown stronger compared to the frail doctor who could hardly carry his own medicine case but that doesn't mean he's made for battle. After all, I fell in love with a man who could save lives, not take them away.

"Let's see here..."

The last time I came this way, Captain Xian took the route from Ning. Ning is the empire east of our Nan Rong. After the conflict, relationships between our two lands have been on better terms; nevertheless, that doesn't mean they'll permit a Southerner to freely ride through their gates. According to this map, the direct route is straight north to Bei Ling's main gates and then turn east toward Man Wan. The other option is to take the old trade route, Jue, and cut diagonally to Man Wan.

"Jue would be faster but... that's probably a bad idea."

"Good to see you've become less reckless. I'm proud."

From the shade of a plum tree, his tall form moves from shadows into the bright afternoon sunlight. The brown steed, whose reins are tied to the tree, is quietly napping, meaning he's been waiting for a while.

"Wh-Wh-What the! D-Dui? How did you beat me here?!"

"The better question is, did you really think I wouldn't know what you were up to?"

"Dui, please. Go back to Pa Xu. I don't want you involved!"

"I can stand my ground."

"That's not why! This is not your fight. In fact, you shouldn't be mixed up in any fighting, Doctor! Saving lives, that's your profession."

"Sometimes saving lives require more than medicine. You can continue to argue and I'll ride ahead to Ming Na or we can ride together. Your choice."

"You—!"

Stubborn, stubborn man! I have no idea how he rode here so quickly when I clearly had a head start. I definitely shouldn't have told him about Ming Na. I can't outrun him, and even if I could, he'll still find me. It's not fair. Well, as long as he's not being fair, neither will I.

The physician tugs at the sleepy creature. After mounting, he aims to take the lead.

"Aren't you doing too much for someone who doesn't even love me?"

Shoulders tense from the sore subject. Dui nearly looks back but catches himself in time. He gives no heed to my provocation; instead, starts forward at a slow trot.

"Hurry or I'll leave you behind."

"Fine, leave me! One man's trash is another man's treasure. Maybe someone else will come along and scoop me up. I'll gladly go with him too, whoever he is, since you don't want me anyway!"

Ugh, that was pathetic. What a terrible plan. I have no idea what badgering him was meant to accomplish. The more I attempt to annoy Dui, the farther apart our distance becomes. At this rate, he'll reach Ming Na before I manage to find Nan Rong's borders.

Chapter 4 – 3

Around a small campfire, Dui made dinner and set aside a comfortable sleeping area for me; a simple mat topped by a grey blanket which has an adorable panda embroidery on the top right corner. He purchased it from Guan's trade shop last year as a joke and it's become my favorite blanket. As usual, Dui's well prepared and silently considerate. He always does little things like this to please me, to make me feel loved and cared for. I've nothing for him.

On the other side of the fire, where he purposefully settled in order to avoid me, the doctor, with his head down, continues to thumb through one of the poultice books borrowed from Master Tai Hung's study. To his left, manuals and scrolls pour out from the overloaded leather satchel, ranging from acupressure to chi control and heart surgery. His studies have shifted more toward traditional medicine recently; Yu Qi's specialty.

"Dui."

"Hmm?"

"I'm sorry."

"Hmm."

"Is that all you have to say? Listen, I shouldn't have disregarded your feelings all this time. I've been conceited, wallowing in my own heartache without much consideration for yours. I guess I was waiting for you to profess your love again before I would admit mine, but you're always taking such good care of me that I've overlooked your messages. It didn't need to be said. I should have returned the appreciation; made you feel loved and wanted."

The booklet in his hands remains on the same page for some time. He shyly casts up half a glance before resuming the task.

"Everything I have done has been of my own free will. You don't need to apologize. I'm not mad, just in disbelief."

"Then what must I do for you to believe me? "

Shoulders rise and lower in the same casual fashion; his head is still toward the book. "I'm sure one of us will come to sense."

"I hope you're not referring to me."

"If you're thus inclined."

"That's just... Fine. I'm sorry and you're right. One of us will eventually come to his senses and forgive the other for being selfish."

He remains silent and continues to thumb through the book. So much for progress. Maybe now is not the time for this. We have a long ride to Ming Na and the challenges waiting on the horizons are still obscured. For now, all I can do is default to my usual comfort and pray.

Chapter 5: The E Mo's Troubles

A week and half later, our horses come upon Ming Na's western gates. The city is about twice the size of an average village with only a handful more residents. Barely have Dui and I dismount, we're both trapped in foreign arms.

"Miss Bao Lai!"

"Master Dui!"

Their voices ring out in unison. The young woman clinging to Dui's neck and the young man whose arms have captured my body are so agonizingly familiar. By the jade color of her eyes, rosy cheeks, and youthful voice, she is undoubtedly Li Li. Her hair's grown and so has her once prepubescent body. She could rival my... well-endowed stature. This young man on the other hand, I'm not certain, but he really couldn't be anyone else.

"Mo Bi, is that you?"

"Of course it is, Miss Bao Lai. Don't you recognize me?"

The smile is there. That may be the only thing left about him that I can recall from our previous encounter. It's been six months and these two have grown like weeds.

"You're so tall, kid! And your voice is so deep. Is that *facial hair*?"

"A-ha! Not a kid anymore, Miss Bao Lai. I'm glad you came. I've been waiting for a long time."

"Sorry, I came as soon as I could. The letter didn't specify. What's going on?"

"Um, well, I'll let the General fill in the details. We've had some trouble and you're the best troublemaker I know so... anyway, I want to show you something."

"General? Which general? H-Hey wait!"

The tall, lanky giant tugs at my wrist without discretion, practically dragging me away from the well-endowed girl still cuddling my Dui. The doctor is shuffling uncomfortably but isn't making much effort to withdraw. I bet she was the E Mo child he cured those many years ago. This display of affection is merely from gratitude. I shouldn't feel jealous, I know that, especially of a fourteen-year-old girl.

"Mo Bi, stop walking so fast! I can't keep up with your long legs. Where are we going?"

"Just a little farther, Miss Bao Lai."

"Are you sure this is all right? I distinctly remember my sendoff last time through a hail of rocks. You're not... taking me to be greeted by another volley, are you?"

"Don't be silly. Once they were back home, the hostages released their grudge against Fa Zhen. Well, against you, anyway. I hope you'll forgive them. In any case, that's why I'd asked you to come. We need Fa Zhen's help. Ah, here we are."

Adjacent a rolled up colorful, though faded tarp, are at least sixty jars filled by green plants dabbed here and there with white flowers and adorned with various colored oblong fruits. The jars are surrounded on three sides by clay and rock walls dug deep into the ground. Several sheets of metal rest against the enclosure's interior. Next to the setup is also a large haystack.

"What is this? Are those... peppers?"

"Pretty aren't they?"

"Yes, they are! Wow! Nights here are freezing! How were you able to cultivate them?"

"Mr. Zhang Tang, I mean, Prime Minister Zhang Tang, helped us put these small growing areas together. It's a combination of modern and traditional techniques the elders passed down. Heat is captured and stored from sunlight. At night, the area is insulated so the plants stay warm. Since the base is low, we're also gathering heat from the earth. Neat, huh? We're making sauces and dried products to sell in Xia Pa. Little by little, our cities are becoming more prosperous. A handful of merchants even visit from time to time. Our people can walk into main cities now with some level of acceptance. He was right, hiding in the desert wasn't the way to preserve our existence. We still have a long way to go before losing our *barbarian* status, but it's a start."

Zhang Tang, former leader of the underground faction, the White Crane Order, was nominated by His Highness He Pi to lead Bei Ling after Wang Liang's fall. The very somber, aloof man on the surface turned out to be much kinder than any charismatic nobleman.

"I'm glad. I'm so... very, very glad!" Despite my attempt to keep composure, my breaking voice is on the verge of shattering into a full sob. I can't believe *that* bad habit is returning.

"What's wrong, Miss Bao Lai?"

"N-Nothing."

"Do you still feel guilty because of Fa Zhen? You shouldn't. You're not him. To me, you're just... Bao Lai."

I think I'm suffering from heatstroke. The day is already warmer than any I've experienced and then these binding arms seizing my waist from behind are rushing blood to my head. His chin is on my shoulder; a bout of warm air brushes against my cheek from a heavy sigh. Apparently, the E Mo are much friendlier than I realized.

"M-Mo Bi. That's inappropriate where I come from."

"It's completely appropriate for lovers."

"Come again?"

"I've waited this long. Don't reject me."

"Uh... Excuse me?"

"Is it that difficult to grasp my love for you?"

"*Hunh*?! *Kid, you're confused!*"

"I'm not a kid."

"No? You're practically half my age! What about Li Li? Aren't you two together?"

"Li Li's my little sister, Miss Bao Lai."

"Wh—but... s-she is?"

"Yes. I thought you knew."

Oh geez. So that's why he looked after her so meticulously in Ji You and also why he returned to Ming Na when Wang Liang's men were taking hostages from the outskirt cities. When we were imprisoned, he kept blushing and I had thought his embarrassment was due to Li Li. Those rosy cheeks were actually meant for me. Then, Li Li isn't in love with Mo Bi and she's at the front gate cuddling my Dui. I see.

"Over my dead body!"

Darn it, this kid is fast! I've barely moved two steps and he's in front of me.

"Miss Bao Lai, wait! At least give me a chance!"

"Mo Bi, you're..."

There's no right way to say this and I don't really know what to say. He's giving me wounded puppy dog eyes. I don't want to hurt Mo Bi even though I'm sure this is just a superficial crush he'll outgrow. However, I didn't come to Ming Na to rob the cradle.

"Unhand the merchandise, boy! The lady's dangerous. Don't make her angry."

Threatening, hard boot stomps against the ground are great contrasts to the teasing interjection. Immediately, Mo Bi straightens up as though called to attention by a superior officer.

"Sir!"

Oh dear Heavens, what is happening in the world? The man I love is being fondled by a well-endowed teenage girl at the western gates, next to me is a boy who seems to think I'm age appropriate, and there a distance away is the man I loved who rejected me for a better woman. I really shouldn't have bothered waking up this morning.

"We've more important things to do than fraternize. Fetch Elder Gui for me, trainee."

"Yes sir!"

And there goes Mo Bi toward the large yurt jutting from the southern end of the city. I was aching for that awkwardness to cease and yet here's another one waiting; one more frightening than a teenage boy's misplaced infatuation. Just the sight of him makes my chest hurts. All the while, my conscience is drowning in guilt.

"When Mo Bi said he would bring a warrior to assist, I never guessed you were she."

"Bai Hu. I... Hi."

"Hey. You seem well."

"I... am. How are you?"

"That depends. Are you and Dui together?"

"Uh..." I don't know why I expected anything less direct. He never spares my nerves.

"Well?"

I can't deny attachment to Dui, because there is something between us, and in a sense, we are together. However, in this state of ambiguity, neither can I affirm what isn't true.

"Not... really."

"How so? You either are or you aren't. Which is it?"

"We're... not—not officially. I mean, I confessed and he... rejected me."

Ugh, that wasn't meant to be said aloud. Albeit Hu brushed me aside for Kai, I still feel miserable and downright disloyal to admit that I love another. Maybe the hardest thing to admit is that I still love him.

The longer those golden eyes are directed at me, the harder my heart is thumping inside my chest. I haven't forgotten our time in An. Every second together is dredging up another memory, another emotion. Now I understand why Dui was angry for the confession. Those three words should never have been said to him when clearly, I've not gotten over Bai Hu.

The stiff line on the Demon General's lips grows wide until the quiet air erupts in sharp laughter. "*Dui* rejected *you*? Oh, that is good!"

"How is that good? I see you haven't changed one bit, insensitive jerk!"

A sweet smile breaks across his face. Hu's callused hand is suddenly on my right cheek. I'd forgotten how gentle his rough hands can be.

"Sorry. You're right, I am a jerk. That's why I've been so miserable."

"You have? Why? Did something happen?"

"My wife left me. How should I feel?"

"She did? How could she? I thought Kai—"

"*You*, oblivious woman. You're still wearing the pink robe. I hope that means *our* attachment isn't lost."

He has some nerve saying that so casually after his infidelity, after having severed our bond for Kai. The million grievances I wanted to scream at him during those days in An are surging from the back of my throat.

I didn't unleash them then because he wasn't the same man I fell for. Hu's two consciousnesses merged as a consequence of his injuries on Mount Chou. From the ordeal, the side of him that despised me remained. The part of him which loved me was erased. But then, if that were true, then why is his hand on my face? The loving gaze is one I have not recognized since before Mount Chou. Could it be?

"Bai Hu?"

"What is it, Wife?" He smiles tenderly, stressing the last word as to affirm his return. "Wife" was a joke nickname that became Hu's term of endearment for me.

Almost every muscle on my body is aching to reach for him. The one in the middle of my chest is left holding them back, and in essence, is slowly splitting in two.

"How can you still call me that? What about Kai?"

Hu looks away, frowning, and then turns back after a long exhale. "We broke up."

"Why?"

"Because it was a mistake."

"And it only took you... half a year to figure that out? I'm impressed."

"Ah! It was long before that, before you even left, sarcastic woman. I'd hope you'd fight for me and when you didn't, I thought you didn't care so I figured pushing you over the edge was the answer. That was when you caught us in bed but nothing happened, I swear. You're... not convinced. Look, after my two halves joined, I felt like a child growing up again but I was inside a man's body so I hurt you as an adult would. Recently, I've caught up to you and... I'm sorry. I was a stupid, stupid man! You loved me, we were living together, and I intentionally kissed someone else. I cheated. I'm so sorry!"

The rigid jaw line, furrowed brows, and heated touch on my cheek make me believe he's telling the truth. There is an undeniable mature air about him that was lacking during our time in An. He has returned to his old self; more so, grown as a person. However, this isn't news I wanted to hear. I'd hoped Hu was happy in his new life with Kai. I'd left under the presumption of having given Hu the happiness he deserved. He's been miserable and now, so am I.

"Bai Hu..."

"That's enough." A hard tug exaggerates the distance from my fawning former paramour. Dui's grip locks tightly around my arm. His face is hard, his eyes cold. He's never been this intimidating.

"Don't treat my wife so roughly."

"She is not your wife."

"She's not yours either. You had your chance and I heard you graciously declined. I'd appreciated if you will remain a gentleman and unhand my lover."

"For nearly the past year, these two hands have taken care of her, and these shoulders were the ones she'd cried on while you spent endless *pretense* nights with another woman to torture Bao Lai. I don't care who you think you are. You don't have the right to walk back into her life and demand priority. Let's go, Bao Lai. We have work to do."

"Wait, Dui! What about Elder Gui—?"

"I've already requested an audience. He'll meet us at sundown."

Chapter 5 – 2

Pain from Hu's expression is seared into my conscience, billowing guilt already overflowing in my heart. Guilt, likewise, was the reason Hu didn't give chase when Dui pulled me away. There was still much left unsaid between us. All the while, there are few choice words I have for Dui. Once we pass the threshold into the guest tent where his equipments are laid, vexation naturally flows.

"What were you trying to do?"

"What do you mean?"

"Don't play dumb! Stop acting jealous when you won't pursue anything between us!"

"I'm not and I thought you won't bring it up anymore."

"I lied, okay?! So, you were right. Maybe... I haven't gotten over Bai Hu and at the first notion of his love returning, I'm feeling hopeful. What now? If you weren't jealous then why did you pull me away? Just admit you love me already!"

He's glowering. That's never a good sign. Dui's grip relaxes and then he moves away.

"Do you know how desperately spoiled you sound? You're far cry from the controlled woman I fell for in An."

"That's because you're driving me insane! Don't chase after me if you don't love me!"

"I'm trying to protect you."

"I don't need your protection!"

"No? Maybe, you've forgotten that man's mistreatment but I haven't. I haven't forgotten the countless times you've cried your eyes out because he'd ignored you for weeks over one misunderstanding. And, I haven't forgotten the nights I spent listening to you cry yourself to sleep after leaving that cheating bastard. He's sorry. Great! I guess that makes every insult to injury forgivable. If you're so certain he's the one then go back to him!"

"*Argh*! Do you realize how *jealous* you sound?! Obviously, you still love me!"

"That doesn't mean I want to be with you."

Outside, a swift sweep of wind lashes against the tent flap and then recedes, inviting silence to encroach upon our standoff, leaving our hearts in disarray. There's torture on his face and resentment in darkened eyes. He's hurt through a pain I can neither grasp nor cure. I've made Dui miserable, the way I ruined Bai Hu's happiness. Every time I fall for someone, I just end up falling on my face instead.

"Sorry."

"You don't have to apologize when you're not at fault, Dui. I'm the one who insisted on following you to Pa Xu. *I'm* sorry. Fact is, I want to help the E Mo. You don't have to stay with me out of obligation or protect me because we're friends. There's a quiet life waiting back in Nan Rong."

"I'm not going anywhere."

He settles onto the mat in the middle of the tent and begins to fumble with the prepared equipment as if to signal that discussions are over. There's nothing here to do but I know the moment I step foot outside, he'll follow to keep me from Bai Hu. These mixed signals are wreaking havoc on my nerves. I can't decide if he's flattering or infuriating. Either way, my only resolve is to sit near the entrance and twiddle my thumbs.

Chapter 5 – 3

"Is anyone else from An coming?"

Hu shakes his head. "Zhang Tang's letter sounded desperate, but from what I gathered, tracking the culprit is most of the work. His Highness could have just sent Qing Hai."

Around the brazier inside Elder Gui's yurt are Mo Bi, Li Li, several elders and elite warriors, along with Bai Hu, Dui, and I. Hu arrived the day prior, seemingly oblivious to the true reason for his assignment. I bet His Highness sent him as a mean to build ties with the Northern tribes. After all, Hu's superior strength is a result of his 'barbarian' blood.

Also in the tent is Elder Ci who serves as translator. Aside from Elder Gui and Ci, the rest have had little to say.

"Where do we start?"

Elder Gui, the man with a beard as long as my hair, strokes the silvery mane in quiet contemplation. With care, his unsteady hand draws a few lines onto the earth with the walking stick, marking circles here and there to portray stars and planetary alignments. In time, the elder looks up, sending a steady gaze around the yurt until landing upon me.

"The stars tell me everything started with you. You are responsible for our troubles, Demon Slayer."

"Hey, now! She just got here today. Bao Lai has nothing to do with those girls!"

Out of habit, the gallant Hu moves to defend, placing a deliberate barrier to divide me from the fidgeting E Mo warriors. Mo Bi was right. Most of the E Mo have overlooked the blood in my veins, the blood passed down from the man who nearly annihilated all the Northern tribes during his campaign to subdue barbaric Demons, though not all. A handful has been furtively conferring their resentment and the methods through which vengeance could be claimed.

I can't blame them. Almost a thousand year after Fa Zhen's campaigns, the tribes are still shunned outcasts. Their lives have been difficult and they have been denied many rights due human beings. A year ago, women and children were seized and taken to Ji You during the conflict. Now, just when ties are beginning to build with the outside world, this atrocity is threatening all progress, pushing the E Mo back into seclusion and ultimately, possible extinction.

Twenty young women have gone missing from the three outskirt cities in the past two months. Four bodies have been found covered in lacerations, stab wounds, trauma to head and genitalia, as well as missing body parts. The E Mo have been keeping their people locked inside the cities until the culprit is found. However, having opened their doors to outsiders, the number of suspects is limitless. Whoever behind this could have left altogether.

Chapter 5: The E Mo's Troubles

Ever since the E Mo's distress was revealed, I've been feeling an indescribable uneasiness, the same uneasiness experienced during my time in Ji You. These couldn't have been random acts of violence which could start and stop on a whim. The person behind this must have an agenda and he or she won't cease until that goal is met. The culprit has not and will not move on. Of this, I feel certain.

"It's okay, Bai Hu. Thank you for your courtesy but I want Elder Gui to explain. What can I do to help the E Mo?"

The old man smiles. With this short signal of approval, the E Mo warriors resume their steady postures. Hu, though still uncertain, ultimately draws back.

"How the past always manages to repeat itself is a mystery. You remind me of another traveler who came here some decades ago, Demon Slayer. Mian Shi Fen was his name. A troublemaker by trade. He too was always ready to meddle in other's affairs without much consideration."

"Really? Mian Shi Fen came *here*? Oh, I love his poetry! He's my favorite poet!"

"If we are thinking of the same person then that is not all he is to you."

"Meaning?"

"Had you walked a different path, his past would have been revealed by another. It is not my place. As such, your eyes are sincere, same as his. I believe you will help us no matter the cost."

"I don't know what that first part means but okay. And, of course I'll help. I didn't come this far just to run away."

"Well said, Demon Slayer. Allow me to apologize on everyone's behalf, to you, to Master Dui, and to General Bai Hu. We have not been entirely candid."

"Whoa! Whoa! Don't do that!"

Those rickety knees are ready to buckle. We three outsiders rush to raise the bowing elder before they give out. He can hardly sit straight. Unnecessary bowing is entirely too taxing at his age.

"Tai Hung's pupils certainly have good manners." The old man laughs and breathes heavily at once while shuffling back into position on the short chair made from an old stump.

"How do you know Master Tai Hung?"

"Don't you mean how does he know we're his pupils?"

The second question, posed by Dui, goes unanswered. Elder Gui looks up, eyes glazed, as though recalling fond memories. "Every young man suffers from wanderlust at one time or other. His wife wasn't particularly happy with his impulsive habits. Kind woman but strict. She chased him from the house with a frying pan after he snuck the boy here for a month without notice... or was it a meat cleaver?"

"Master Tai Hung was married?! What boy?! Did he have a son?!"

My companions have been shocked silent. I can't keep from running my mouth. In one fell swoop, everything I ever thought I knew about my master crumbled. Master Tai Hung was an old codger. That's all he was to me. It makes sense that he had another life during those younger years but that never occurred to me. To me, he was perpetually an old man, my master.

"Have I said too much?" Elder Gui gazes back innocently.

"N-No, I want to know more! Who's his son? Where is he? Where's his wife? How come they never visited the old man?"

"Those things are beyond me, Demon Slayer."

"That's a load of crap! Use your star map thingy and figure it out! I have to find them! They'd want to know what happened to their loved one!"

"Bao Lai, show a bit of modesty when speaking to an elder."

Leave it up to Dui to be prim and proper. Out of us three, Master Tai Hung liked him best. That much I still remember.

"That's all right, young master. I'm afraid I can't find the answers. Their stars have long fallen."

"Oh... you mean..."

Elder Gui nods sadly as a mean of offering condolences. No wonder Master Tai Hung's family never visited and also maybe why he was such a cranky old codger for as long as I knew him. I hope he's with them, wherever they are.

"My apologies for the upset. That was not my intention. Let us return to the matter at hand, my friends."

"Yes, please." Dui insists. "What have you kept from us, Elder?"

The old man, wiping his brows with a long sleeve, marks a few more lines onto the earth. "Peril befell the E Mo in more ways than one. Shortly before our first girl went missing, another poor soul was lost in Man Wan. Governor Lu Su's daughter, Cai Yun, was discovered slaughtered in her own bedroom. The killer left an artifact behind, one that points to the E Mo."

"So... Did one of you do it?"

"Bao Lai," Dui mutters gruffly under his breath. He's not happy again.

"No, please be as direct as you wish. That is the only way to develop trust. We asked the same from each of our people. Everyone was accounted for during the time of the murder and each has sworn an oath of truth to the great Cao Sung. The artifact is E Mo but it does not belong to us. The E Mo was not behind this murder."

"Governor Lu is less convinced?"

"Naturally. Prime Minister Zhang Tang is the only reason that we have not suffered backlash for the unfortunate event. So we thought, until our girls and women started disappearing."

"And you think the Governor is behind this?"

"No. I don't. He is a grieving father. His wrath is against our men, not our women. Governor Lu has personally come to speak with our elders and he's as saddened by the loss of our girls as he is for his own daughter. Even so, until the culprit is found, fingers will be pointed at our people and someone has to pay."

"Well, I am sorry about his daughter but what exactly do you mean by someone has to pay? Is he just going to punish some random person?"

"He intends to arrest and *interrogate* every young man until one or more confesses."

"I won't let that happen." Bai Hu's seething rage is so palpable, it's nigh tangible. His large hands are fists. The sudden proclamation claims undivided attention from the other warriors. In spite of the language barrier, men of war seem to share mutual understanding. To the E Mo elites, since inception, the Northern courts and their affiliates have wished for the tribes' demise, while this general, a stranger who owes nothing to the E Mo, doesn't hesitate to take arms for their protection. The Demon General is more so a saint. That respect which I've witnessed from his peers and subordinates in Nan Rong is wholly mirrored by the men present, if not more.

"How would Zhang Tang ever allow that?" Dui also enters conversation though his anger is more subdued.

"Prime Minister Zhang Tang knows better than to make enemies of his allies. Politics require tradeoffs. One innocent man's life will console a grieving father and make a country feel safe. And you, General, should not let your emotions guide your weapon. Killing hundreds to save a few is not good judgment. After your departure, we must remain."

"Then doesn't that mean we're back at the beginning? We just need to find the culprit."

"Yes, Demon Slayer, but it is not that easy. We have sent our best trackers and all have returned empty handed. Within the month, Governor Lu's men will arrive to seize ours. To top things off, we are still unable to keep our women safe."

"Wished you'd sent for help sooner but I guess I don't understand why you sent for me anyway, Elder.

Can't the stars tell where this person is and wouldn't it be more beneficial for a large number of soldiers to aid in the search? I'm sure His Highness He Pi can spare a few hundred men."

"Our few hundred men have walked this desert far longer than any imperial soldier and have likewise failed. I do not know more than the stars will reveal and they are pointing to you. Through a heroic act, you have made an enemy."

"An enemy who's targeted your people?"

"Yes. An enemy who despises us equally. Fa Zhen's blood flows strongly through your veins, and through him, you will find his blood."

"Erm... What does that mean?"

"I think Elder Gui is implying the culprit is another Demon Slayer."

"The healer is correct," Elder Gui nods thoughtfully. "After five went missing from Yue Na and Er Na, all three cities have been vigilant. Since then, fifteen more have been taken from under our noses, some at night from their tents, others seemingly disappeared into thin air during midday. Our trackers have not been successful. Our tacticians could not outmaneuver this phantom. Our warriors' massive strengths were useless. There was naught we could do against an enemy of this caliber."

"How is that possible? Haven't you set up watchtowers and traps? What about patrols and alert systems? Nan Rong's regiment uses a series of devices. I can set them up here."

"All efforts have been useless, General." Ci takes a step forward. He stands adjacent Elder Gui, a position which quickly makes several pairs of watchful eyes dart about uncomfortably. "Though, it does seem we are of the same mindset. These feats were not possible, not unless the culprit can bend the flow of time. Security doesn't matter when faced with the Demon Slayer's ability."

A ripple of dread sweeps over the tent, turning almost every face pallid. Fa Zhen's descendents are numerous but to be noted as a Demon Slayer requires certain ability, an ability that could decimate an entire army if honed properly. From what I can recall, the ability is mainly passed down from father to son. Daughters like me who inherit the trait are anomalies. The majority can't effectively wield their gifts, if at all.

The skill requires grievous exchange on the wielder's part. To have used Tian Ji Zhong Shi Yan that many times in two months without faltering probably means our opponent's ability naturally overpowers mine. Aside Bai Hu, no one thus far has been able to break through my skill. This difficult task is nearing impossibility.

Scratching his head uneasily, Bai Hu clears his throat in hopes of breaking the mounting tension. "Be that as it may, any security measure is better than none. Let's say we can't keep this person from entering, there are methods to force a trail."

"We E Mo believe in the will of Heaven, General. The stars have pointed to Miss Bao Lai. Her blood is our greatest advantage and our best security."

"How's that?" Hu moves closer to my side, furrowing his brows at the languid Ci.

"It's as Elder Gui said, General, her blood can lead us to the other Demon Slayer." Elder Ci bows politely.

"Can't you be a bit more helpful? Bao Lai can't keep from getting lost inside a city, tracking down a killer in the middle of a desert is out of her league."

He's trying to be nice but that was a low blow. During my second day as Hu's ward, I came into trouble during an accidental excursion down the Red Light District. Although I managed to fend off three thugs, the sight of Hu coming for me that night is engraved in my mind, still. Up until then, I'd never felt so relieved and inexplicably happy to have his companionship. It might have been that moment when I began falling for him.

My heart is hurting again. Half is aching from Hu's loving sidelong glance, the other half is aching from Dui's frown. The three of us have been through much together since our days at Tian Mao Yi. It's difficult to keep distant memories from dredging up. I know they must be going through the same.

"Care to venture a guess, Demon Slayer?" Elder Gui casts a direct smile.

"I'm... not sure. During the conflict, our common enemy was Wang Liang but I don't think he had my ability else the war would have easily fallen to his favor."

"What about Ji You? Didn't you say that's where you met the E Mo hostages?"

Dui's incautious mention of Ji You abruptly twists Mo Bi's placidness into deep rage. The sordid memories overtaking him are irrepressible. He looks to Li Li. She's not in any better mood.

"You may have a point, Dui, but those soldiers were captured by Qing Hai and Captain Xian. They were handed over to Zhang Tang in the aftermath and imprisoned. Besides, when I used Tian Ji Zhong Shi Yan, none of the soldiers retaliated. Shouldn't the one who shared my ability have been able to match my sword?"

"Possibly, the culprit wasn't aware of his own ability. Yours didn't awaken until Bai Hu was injured on Mount Chou. Maybe through experiencing yours, his was awakened."

"You really did save me on Chou?" Hu's tender words suddenly shift the tense atmosphere to something sweet. "I thought old man Zhuang exaggerated."

"Well, uh, D-Dui was really the one who did most of the work before Master Zhuang showed up. I just swung a sword indiscriminately."

"So, you did save me." Hu reasserts with vaguely, a little more force.

Those gentle eyes make my heart takes off like a rocket. A burst of flames feels seared onto my cheeks.

Why couldn't he have been this sweet during my last days in An? I'd left under the notion that Hu was happy without me and that I could support Dui. Neither turned out to be true. I wonder if I've ever done anything right. The E Mo are in trouble due to a powerful enemy whose latent, deadly ability I'd unknowingly invoked. What if through fixing these mistakes, something worse will happen?

"Do not doubt yourself, Demon Slayer. Once that deadly poison is consumed, it will wreak havoc, not only to yourself but also to your allies."

"Was I mouthing my thoughts?"

"Not at all," Elder Gui chuckles. "Your eyes are very sincere. I do not need to know what you are thinking in order to know your thoughts. There's conflict boiling in your heart; past and present tugging at once. You wish to suppress the turmoil lest it tears you apart. Don't. Nothing is solved from avoidance. To grow as a person, sometimes it is necessary to explore alternatives that which before you would not dare discover, to gain that which otherwise would be unattainable."

"I, uh, appreciate the words of wisdom, Elder, but you're actually making things harder for me."

Upon Elder Gui's guidance, Dui and Hu immediately jump to their silent glaring contest. The former won't accept my affections but neither will he permit me too close to the latter, who in turn seeks to rekindle what we've lost. To keep from avoidance and to explore all alternatives would mean to break the restraint I've placed over my heart for Bai Hu. I don't know if I can do that. I don't want to lose Dui, even if he's not mine to lose.

"Nothing worth having comes easy. Trust in yourself, Demon Slayer, and let your heart lead the way. By the end of this conflict, the answer will come to you."

"Well, now, you sound full of it just like Master Huan from Tian Mao Yi. Actually, you look a bit like him. You're not... related to him, are you?"

"Bao Lai, that's impolite."

"He looks just like him though! Don't you think so too?"

"I'm his brother," Elder Gui nods before Dui could reply.

"R-Really?"

"No. You are more gullible than I imagined, Demon Slayer, and temperamental too. I take back what I said. It must have been due luck you've made it this far. I'd be surprised if you could find your way out of a hat!" Wizen cheeks tint red. Incessant cackles fill the entire yurt. His eyes roll to the ceiling, on the verge of popping from their sockets. The long beard waves back and forth as though agreeing with the rude old man.

"You're a rude old man!"

"Bao Lai!"

"What?!"

"That's inappropriate."

"Stop correcting me, Dui!"

"I will when you stop behaving like a child."

"*Me?* Oh, I get it. I'm glad you're finally free from your delusions, Doctor. Sorry if I'm not the *controlled woman* you thought I was. Deal with it! I didn't ask you to come!"

Chapter 5 – 4

Well, that was embarrassing. Aside from having made a complete ass of myself, I might have ruined the good doctor's reputation and now I can't go back into the yurt. The meeting is probably over. I guess if I hadn't stormed out, I would know. As much as I hate to admit it, Dui was right. My self-control has completely gone out the window. An inexplicable panic has come over me; more so, a sense of dread. It's difficult to think straight anymore. Every little thing is making me angry.

"You'll catch cold out here."

He plops a fur coat around my shoulders and then settles adjacent on the stone bench. A faint glimmer of sunlight remains from over the horizon. The air is noticeably chilly.

"Thanks. What about you?"

"I'll manage," he scoffs. "That was quite the scene."

"Did you come to lecture me too, Xiao Meow?"

"Heh. Never thought I'd hear that again! You should know by now. Xiao Mao is always on your side, Little Hung."

Our old nicknames from Tian Mao Yi. Unlike his name, Hu wasn't much of a tiger twenty years ago, so the monks called him Little Cat or Xiao Mao. I called him Xiao Meow. Everyone called me Little Hung, after my master.

"Good. I'm glad. You know, after you left temple, I never thought I'd see Xiao Meow again either. That day we *ran* into one another on the road near Kou, you knew it was me, right?"

"Until your attitude surfaced, I wasn't certain."

"But then you were certain and you still didn't tell me."

"It was your fault for forgetting."

"How would I have recognized you? I grew one foot taller. You turned into a giant!"

"And that's precisely why I didn't admit the truth. I was a shrimp who couldn't win one fight against Little Hung. Not exactly the manly image I thought you should perceive."

"Ha! You were a shrimp. Half my height, as I recall."

"That's some exaggeration." Hu frowns, and then sometime after, smiles to himself.

Silence slowly creeps in between us but it's not uncomfortable. Having him near somehow makes everything less daunting. Twenty years ago, Xiao Meow was my best friend. For a time, we were inseparable despite daily spats which usually ended with one or both our heads smacked by Master Tai Hung. When Master Zhuang removed Hu from temple without any notice, I nearly went mad from waiting for him daily by the main road. We were only friends then. I can't imagine what he must have gone through in An.

"Hey, Hu. I'm sorry for having left without telling you. Hope you weren't worried. I thought about sending letters but honestly, I didn't think you'd care."

"Yeah, well... you couldn't have been more wrong."

"Are you blushing?"

"Quiet. The Demon General doesn't blush."

"Uh-huh. He's just a big fat liar then?"

"Hmph. I figured you'd returned home with *him*. Qing Hai confirmed that."

"You sent Qing Hai to track me? Stalker! No wonder he wasn't surprised to see me in Pa Xu!"

"*I* didn't stalk you, Qing Hai did, though now I kind of wish I had. You two really aren't together, huh?"

"Rub it in my face, why don't you?"

"That wasn't what I meant. Should have known better. I can't leave you alone with him for a moment without any funny business."

"Dui's not that type of person."

"I meant you. Twenty years ago, you were ogling Tai Hung's tall, lanky apprentice. Why else would your short friend have goaded you into giving him a hard time?"

"You did what?"

"As I recall, my mere suggestions were taken overboard by an overzealous girl who confused attraction for dislike. Maybe now you'll understand my overreaction when it comes to Dui."

"I've... liked Dui for that long?"

"Hmm. Apparently, some things never change. The more he ignored your provocations, the more you taunted him. I almost felt bad for him. Almost."

"I tortured Dui for two years straight based on your recommendations?"

"Sure. So long as you two were on bad terms, you were mine alone."

"That's just... downright manipulative. Poor Dui!"

"Dui? What about me? You'd be surprised how difficult it was to influence an oblivious girl."

Until this moment, I never knew just how much Bai Hu has accomplished to keep me for himself. His manipulation wasn't exactly noble but was somehow strangely sweet. His obsession for me bordered Kai's obsession for him. Slightly frightening, but again, perplexingly adorable.

"Now that the *cat's out of the bag*, your tactics are rendered moot, Xiao Meow."

"Think so? I don't need base tactics when you can't even seduce him after a year together. Isn't it obvious? You'll only find compatibility with one particular man."

"Who would that be? Certainly not the man who tossed me aside, in Dui's care at that, over one misunderstanding. Nor the man who tried to kill me in Bei Ling, and then without one apology, took Kai to our bed."

"Ah! You'll hold it over me for the rest of my life, won't you? I said I was sorry. I wasn't myself, okay? Not entirely. Just a stupid, *stupid* confused man-child!"

There's regret in his woeful eyes. There are tears misting over mine. I thought I'd let go of my resentment, but I haven't, and maybe I haven't because a part of me still loves Bai Hu—will always love him, regardless. Elder Gui said that in order to settle the turmoil in my heart, I can't give into avoidance. These repressed feelings need to be explored. The part of me that wants to is held back by an equal part that refuses to betray Dui.

In the midst of the cold atmosphere, a large, gentle hand overlaps mine, providing a rush of warmth. The sweet face peering down is just as comforting. "Why don't you come back with me after this is over and let me make things up to you?"

"Eh... Wh-What are you talking about? That's... very funny."

"I mean it. I'll make you happy—much happier than before—and this time, permanently."

He's not joking. In fact, I can't recall a time he's been more serious. I can't lie and say that I'm not happy by the offer. More than happy, my heart's beating out of my chest. The answer should come effortlessly. Dui made his intentions perfectly clear. Maybe I need to stop chasing after phantoms and reach for that which is tangible. Maybe I need to take the easy route. So why can't I? Why can't I agree? Would taking Hu's offer when my heart is wounded mean that I'd love him by default, the very reason Dui resents me?

"Bao Lai? What's your answer?"

"Oh! I-I, uh... um—"

"I need to talk to you. It's urgent."

Why am I getting the feeling that Bai Hu is not the only one stalking me? His interruptions seem really calculated. At least they're giving me an excuse to delay this conversation.

"S-Sure. Hold on, Dui. I, uh, I have to go. Here's your coat back. Stay warm. Good night, Bai Hu."

"Wait, Bao Lai. This isn't over. There's still plenty of time. Think things through carefully and give me an answer when you're ready. Until then, don't be a stranger. We're meant for each other. I will make you fall in love with me all over again."

Those last words may have been for me but there was also an inherent challenge directed at Dui. The two lock eyes, neither willing to back down from the absurd staring contest. At this rate, we'll all freeze to death.

"Dui. You wanted to speak to me?"

Frowning, his jaw clenches. Ultimately, the doctor resigns when my hands press against his chest. He looks down once and then starts away.

Chapter 5 – 5

"I thought I told you to be careful around him."

Half my body is still outside of the tent flap and already, he's griping.

"We were just talking. What is it you want?"

Letting out a long exhale, Dui settles onto one of the low chairs by a writing table. Scarcely do troubled grey eyes dart up, his attention swings away to another side of the tent. "*Sorry* if I interrupted but this is more important. When was the last time you used Tian Ji Zhong Shi Yan?"

"Since... the raid on Sai Mi."

"That's what I thought." He lets out another exhale.

As usual, I haven't considered any repercussion. The last time the ability was invoked, my heart nearly gave out. Yu Qi, Dui's elder brother, used a chi control technique to block my heart from exploding. He warned not to use the skill until the month was over. That was a while ago and I haven't chanced it since. There's no telling what could happen. If the culprit does turn out to be another Demon Slayer, invoking the skill will be unavoidable. Should I fail to dispatch him quickly, the same outcome from last time can be expected, except without Yu Qi to save me, I won't have to worry about answering Hu's proposal.

"Don't use it."

"I don't think I have a choice, Dui."

"We don't know for sure that he's using Tian Ji Zhong Shi Yan to take victims. He might not even possess the ability. There's no point risking it until we're certain."

"And if we're certain?"

"Then go home. Live your life out peacefully. I'll find another way."

"You should know me better than that. Besides, Bai Hu is here. He managed to break through my skill and walked away unscathed. I won't be fighting alone. And before you say that I'm discounting you again, I'm not. This isn't your fight. I might have caused this. Why don't *you* return home and pretend I never followed you to Pa Xu?"

"This wasn't your fault. Elder Gui was wrong to put these atrocities on your shoulders. You've already saved the E Mo once. Let me. Go with the Demon. Now's your chance. It's not too late to have the life you've wanted with him."

"Are you kidding me? First you ignored me and then when I tried to give you space, you followed me here. Now you're pushing me toward Hu, when each time we're close, you tug back. Which is it?"

"I don't want to discuss this."

"Well, I do! Just when I think I understand what you want, you go out of your way to give mixed signals. Not long ago in Feng Jia, you called me a hypocrite but aren't you acting the same?!"

"M-M-Master Dui?"

Wonderful! Another meddling watcher, this one carries an odd obsession for Dui. She's too much of a child to win his favor. Apparently, Li Li's come to the same conclusion. Following the soft call, she nervously peeks into the tent. The former braided pigtails have been pulled into a neatly braided bun. There's rouge on cheeks and balm on cherry lips. Her clothes have changed to pieces typically seen on mature ladies. In her hands is a tray of food clearly prepared particularly for Dui. Everything is plated so prettily on decorated bowls and plates. Even the teacup is impressive. The scent wafting from the dishes are intoxicating. Not only is she young, pretty and pure, Li Li is also a *controlled woman* and a good cook. I can't believe I'm jealous of a fourteen-year-old.

"Am I interrupting?"

Despite lack of response, Li Li saunters in and places the tray on the table, then proceeds to take the seat adjacent. Tea is poured for the doctor and the many dishes are laid onto the table. The way she fusses over him is a sore reminder of the times he fussed over me. Dui's taken really good care of me. Until witnessing her friendly display, it wasn't apparent that this is how he should have been treated all along. I've truly been an ungrateful, spoiled brat.

"Miss Bao Lai, dinner's ready. Why don't you join the others in the common area? That's located east from here, toward the center."

I suppose that's cue for me to leave. Dui's not making any attempt to keep me. I might as well withdraw.

Chapter 6: Summit in Er Na

"Have you not found your way out of the hat, my child?" Elder Gui, looking over his shoulder with a genial smile, chuckles.

I hadn't noticed he was there. I was walking with head tilted down into the tall collar to avoid bitterly cold air from nipping at my nose. Elder Gui is used to this climate and his face isn't any less red.

"Very funny, old man. It's freezing. Why are you outside?"

"The cold is not a bother. There are only so many moons left before this old man will cease to feel everything, including the cold, so he intends to enjoy as many as possible. What about you?"

"Can't sleep. Actually, I'm on my way over to the cultivation area. Thought I'd see how the pepper plants fare, mainly to take my mind off things."

"Something bothering you?"

"This entire ordeal has me on edge. I... don't know what I'm supposed to do; or maybe, what I can do. Finding one faceless criminal is difficult enough but one who's also seemingly invisible too? Where do we even start?"

"From the beginning, I imagine."

"Well, aren't you a great help?"

"That's why I'm an elder." The wrinkled smile has a hint of boyishness which never left him. If I hadn't learned about his other life, I'd find it difficult to imagine Elder Gui and the serious Master Tai Hung were ever friends.

"I think you know more than you lead on, Elder. I mean, you can read stars. Why would they tell you some things and keep the rest to themselves?"

"Life would be rather uninteresting with nothing to discover, don't you think?"

"Boredom is a bearable exchange for human lives."

"And would those lives be worth living if they were to discover fate is destiny and freewill is merely an illusion? Would they be contented to know we're all puppets on strings, living and dying as the Heavens ordain?"

"Are you saying the outcome of this conflict has already been decided?"

"Speak with ten elders and you'll have ten different answers," he shrugs. "I was taught to accept fate and the ambiguity of life. Knowing everything won't change anything, especially if revelation is preordained. All that will accomplish is to mitigate appreciation of life. For instance, were I to know there are ten moons left before my departure, the tenth moon is the only I'll bother to value; though, with little success. The other nine would be spent in melancholy or reckless self-endangerment; all in fearful expectation of the tenth. Instead, I am allowed to enjoy every moon until my last, treasuring each moment left."

"Hmm. Well, that sounds great and all but by that logic, even if I leave now, the outcome would be the same."

"True. If you leave now then you are meant to leave and if you stay then you are meant to stay."

"Do I even have a choice?"

"Certainly. Any choice you make is the choice you are meant to make."

"*That's not helpful at all!* If everything I choose to do is that which I was meant to do, and each action is also as fate ordains, then freewill is nonexistent, or that each action becomes the will of fate as it occurs. Heaven is merely watching, coining every action and inaction a fraction of fate."

"So you do understand."

"No, I don't! That's completely senseless! Crimes have been committed. The Heavens know the person responsible. No matter what I do, it is fate, so what harm could there be to tell me who is behind this? That shouldn't change anything!"

Roundabout logic is illogically to me. Besides that, my head hurts. I'm not used to this type of mental exertion. Ever since the end of the Nan Rong – Bei Ling conflict, I've not had to use my head.

During the conflict, there were times I didn't know if I would ever again see Bai Hu or Dui. Somehow we muddled through things and came out unscathed on the other side of the abyss. Whether that was due fate or choice, many things in life would be different if the conflict had been resolved from the very beginning through Wang Liang's demise. For one, Dui and I would not have had the last six months together. Feng Jia would have likely remained the destitute country that it was, tension between Nan Rong and Ning wouldn't have improved, and there wouldn't be this mutual understanding of peace across all five countries. Maybe ambiguity *is* meant to fuel discovery. I hate to admit it. He might actually have a point. Besides, Elder Gui wouldn't let his people suffer. He must not know the killer's identity. Yelling won't change that.

"S-Sorry."

"Hmm? Never apologize for being yourself, my child."

"Well, I'm not exactly myself at the moment. I'm... anxious and confused."

"About?"

"Everything."

"That is a quite a burden," Elder Gui chortles airily. "Maybe I can help. You weren't really outside clearing your mind, were you? You wish to think that were the case but that is not the reason why your sleep was restless. He's on patrol at the south wall."

"W-Who are you talking about?"

"The Demon General, the man you wish to avoid in this unavoidable fashion. Same as each path you do not take, the answer is undiscoverable."

"I... don't think that's any of your business."

Laughing at my expense, Elder Gui's shaky hand rummages inside the large coat pocket for two lozenges. "Oh! To be young and in love! I, too, apologize. Last evening's uncalled for provocation was purposeful on my part.   I intended to see who would be more distraught over your retreat from the yurt. My, it was against all expectations. Want to know?"

"Y-Yes...?"

"Come closer and I'll tell you."

Placing the extra lozenge into my palm, Elder Gui leans in. The cold air's taken a toll. His voice is now a raspy whisper.

However, just as I thought the answer to my aching heart would be resolved, the mean old man refuses to divulge his secret until the victims are found, which makes me think I was right, he is full of it.

Chapter 6 – 2

Last night, my walk to the southern wall was paused by Elder Ci who brought both trouble and reward. The former was news from Er Na. The latter, a totem, bounded in leather, with intricate pattern carved throughout the shiny black stone. It's much like the relic I once used to induce Tian Ji Zhong Shi Yan, which was stolen before Ji You, except this totem has the reverse effect. Blessed by the elders who came before, this piece is said to dispel the Demon Slayer's advantage. The problem though, is that there hasn't been a true Demon Slayer to validate the artifact's use. Dui was adamant in keeping me from inducing Tian Ji Zhong Shi Yan lest my heart gives out. And so, for now, the totem is merely a nice bauble hung around my neck.

"Good luck, Master Dui! Please, stay safe and come back to me!" Li Li swings thin arms around Dui's shoulders, nearly in tears as though she were sending her husband away to battle. He makes no attempt to part.

"Ahem. That's uh... that's quite enough, you two. Dui, are you coming?" Staying here means he'd be in safe hands. At the same time, I don't want anyone else's hands on him. Secretly, I'm glad he's so stubborn.

"Yes, let's get going."

"Just a minute! Here, I made this for you, Master Dui." Cheerfully picking up the flower woven basket near her feet, Li Li presents the token affectionately. "There's a light cover to keep from sunburn. Just in case, I packed an ointment too. Oh, and there's that bread you liked so much and plenty of tonics to keep hydrated."

"Thank you. That's very thoughtful."

"Anything for you, Master Dui. You've been so kind to everyone in Ming Na, especially me. After your last departure, I was worried we'd never meet again. I've waited so long for your return. Once everything settles, why don't you stay a while?"

"Whoa there!"

Who taught this girl to flirt so casually? I thought she was innocent but running fingers up and down his arm in that manner, the fluttery eyelashes and cherry smile... she's perfectly mimicking a deliberate, calculated, matured woman.

"The sun is exceptionally vigorous today. It's getting hotter by the second. Save pleasantries for later. Let's move out, Dui!"

Dui was nearly tugged away from the disgustingly romantic scene when another equal force seizes his free arm. Li Li's a lot stronger than she looks.

"What are you doing, Li Li? Dui and I have to go."

"You're not fooling anyone, Miss Bao Lai. I appreciate what you did for me in Ji You, I really do, but I don't care much for your childish interruptions."

"Excuse me?"

"Every moment with Master Dui is special to me. I won't concede to you or anyone else less qualified."

"And you think you're more qualified than me?"

"Unquestionably. There is not one aspect in which you have me beat. Not in beauty, talent, and certainly not in loyalty. Even my astrological compatibility with Master Dui is most auspicious."

"Is that so? Hmm, well, how about... *you're fourteen and he's thirty-one!*"

"Actually, my birthday hasn't passed. I'm still thirty."

"Quiet Dui!"

"Don't bark at Master Dui! How can you not know his birthday? That is the most special day of the year, the day he came into this world!"

"Oh, please! Spare me your off-the-cuff, superficial nonsense!"

"My birthday is nonsense? Thank you. It's nice to know how highly you think of me."

"Wh... N-No, that's not what I meant! Dui. Dui! *Wait!*"

As the handsome doctor moves away, his lovely worshipper follows suit, leaving behind the crazy woman who's on the verge of pulling out all her hair. Why do I suddenly feel like the villain in this love tale?

"Miss Bao Lai. Be careful." Of all the bad timing! Here comes another to impose the villain's path with big round puppy eyes.

"Uh, t-thanks, Mo Bi. Be a good boy and look after everyone, okay?"

"How many times do I have to say it? I'm not a boy anymore, Miss Bao Lai! When you come back, I'll show you how much of a man I've become!"

"Watch it, kid! No one lays hands on the lady while I'm around. Got it?" Hu moves in between, shoulders squared and muscles flexed. He's practically an alpha come to put the cub in his place.

"Don't flaunt your authority, General. You can't tell me what to do. Ouch!"

Now that was unexpected. On impulse, Hu and I rub our heads in unison along with the wincing Mo Bi. Elder Gui in turn, is staring with raised eyebrows.

"Why did you two rub your heads?"

"Oh... ha ha! It was just so painfully nostalgic. Xiao M—I mean Hu and I—often had our heads smacked in the same fashion by Master Tai Hung. That old coot scarred us for life."

"Pfff. At least it was only Tai Hung for you. Old man Zhuang smacked me too."

"That's because most of the time when we were in trouble, it was all your fault. You were a bad influence!"

Hu sticks out his tongue, the usual rebuttal whenever he has no argument or as a mean to point fingers at me. Back then, it usually followed with our heads smacked by Master Tai Hung while goody two-shoe Dui stood aside and shook his head.

"The General is so juvenile, Miss Bao Lai. Why don't you spend time with me? *Oww!*"

"Save this love... pentagon... for later." Elder Gui sighs in unison with his flying palm. "You've heard the news from Ci, another body was found near Er Na. Another life was lost."

For the tenth time this morning, Elder Gui looks to the sky in search of revelation, only to shake his head disappointedly from another thwarted attempt.

"One warning before you go. Elder Sa is... a strong-willed woman, yes, that would be a nice way to put it. Take her guidance to heart, not so much her words. Now then, make haste, my friends. May Heaven guide you."

Chapter 6 – 3

Er Na is situated between Ming Na and Yue Na. Unlike her sister cities, Er Na has more advanced constructs. There are houses spaced far apart and built rather low, some having a small, gated yard similar in fashion to those quarters in Bi Xi—the Nan Rong village situated at the base of Mount Chou—Bai Hu's hometown. In the middle of Er Na are multiple tall buildings, two of which are a school and a hospital. Situated at the center of these buildings is a courtyard overlooked by a large statue of a tall, broad-shouldered man wielding a long spear. His jaw is rigid. His eyes are kind. There's something eerily familiar about that face.

On the southeastern end, a large cultivated area is reserved, built very much like that of Ming Na, though twice as large and with a drip irrigation system fully equipped. As for the people, who are dressed in noticeably more vibrant colors than E Mo living in the other cities, my foreign tongue is familiar to some degree, especially with the youths. Er Na is as advanced as any modern city.

"Erm... where is Elder Ci? He was right beside me a moment ago."

"Looks like he ditched us for popularity," Hu smirks.

The General points toward a group of young men gathered near the base of the large statue. They flock to the genial elder, chatting as excitedly as had students from Tian Mao Yi around Master Zhuang when he came to give lessons. Master Zhuang was a celebrity though, even outside temple, for his valor during the Hei San and Bai He Campaigns.

The group looks to us three, waving kindly with smiles abound on bright, cheerful faces. Considering the unfortunate reason for our sudden appearances in Er Na, Elder Ci must have a certain way to rally morale. Shortly after, their conversation resumes, as lively as before.

"Why *is* he suddenly so admired?"

"What? Jealous Dui?" Hu smacks the doctor's arm jokingly.

Dui flinches from having been distracted. "Surprised. During my last stay in Ming Na, Ci was practically ignored. He hardly spoke to anyone aside from Elder Gui and kept mostly to himself in the archive yurt."

"People change." Hu replies.

"Yes, usually for a reason."

"Maybe he was tired of being alone, who knows? Are you suddenly suspicious?"

"No. I said surprised."

"Shh! He's coming over, you two."

"So what?"

Frowning, Hu's protective arm lands across my shoulder. Dui brushes it off and then we're left glancing awkwardly at one another while Ci parts from his crowd of admirers.

"I'm sorry, my friends. That was rude of me. I didn't intend to leave you stranded. I just thought it was an excellent opportunity to uncover additional information before our meeting. What's this then? It seems I've raised a few eyebrows."

"Not at all, Elder. We were just—"

"We were wondering why you're such a popular guy," Hu smacks Dui's arm again.

"Oh, well. I wouldn't say popular." Ci smiles bashfully. "I'm one of the youngest elders, you see, and sometimes young men need another young man's perspective. I'm not their age by all means, but I'm much closer than, say—Elder Sa or Elder Ke."

"That makes sense. Old people are usually set in their ways. I loved Master Tai Hung but he was difficult to talk to sometimes—most of the time. I was close to Master Lo Han because of his easygoing nature."

"I can't believe you still remember that snake!"

"Master Lo Han is... complicated."

Actually, Master Lo Han tried to kill me during the Bei Ling – Nan Rong conflict. There was rationale behind his actions; none of which Hu would ever accept.

In fact, Hu doesn't know about that event. I had no idea his opinion of Lo Han was so base.

"Sure, because you always saw him through rose-colored lenses. He's a snake, Bao Lai. A snake through and through!"

"Lo Han is of little consequence, you two." Dui cuts in matter-of-factly. "If you don't mind, Elder, did the young men say anything about the recent murder?"

"I'm afraid they're not much help," Ci's head shakes disappointedly. "They were, however, ecstatic to see foreign faces. Ming Na is used to having imperial visitors. Er Na and Yue Na, well, I can't say the same. Don't become alarmed if some older citizens are less than welcoming. Prejudice and intolerance are aspects built from age and experience. The E Mo have faced much hardship. It's not truly their fault. For me, the future lies in the hands of youths."

"Wow, that's very forward-looking, Elder."

"I am only doing my part to ensure the E Mo's future."

Bowing gracefully, Ci extends an inviting hand. "Shall we go, my friends?"

Chapter 6 – 4

By the time our party arrive in the large hall located north of the centered courtyard, elders, warriors and those respected alike from Er Na and Yue Na have already gathered. The building is massive enough to hold over two hundred with plenty of room to spare. Our small party had anticipated a private conversation, not this summit, which is making me increasingly uncomfortable for more reasons than one.

I had hoped to remain inconspicuous by dawdling near the main door but it didn't take long for a woman to point out the Demon Slayer. Ironically, her kind greeting brought tension to the room. Half of those present are full of smiles; the other half are reaching for their daggers.

One tall soldier moves to my defense. At the sight of his broad shoulders and keen eyes, those in opposition quickly lower their hands. A few even bow their heads.

"Um... What's going on?"

"Your friend is the spitting image of Chief Cao Sung," Elder Ci, who came on behalf of Ming Na's council and to act as interpreter, replies rather loudly as if to ensure the dissidents would realize my ties to Hu.

"That's the second time I've heard that name. Who is he?"

"Cao Sung is our hero." Elder Ci continues. "Almost a thousand years ago, Chief Cao Sung led the defense against Fa Zhen's massacre. At one point, the two sides were at stalemate. Fa Zhen's army continued to decimate ours through rising reinforcements. Our numbers slowly dwindled until Chief Cao Sung had little left to protect. Regardless, the Southern courts, as well as Fa Zhen, recognized his strength and honor. To bargain for our lives, he bravely forfeited his own. He's the only reason we haven't been exterminated, which is more than can be said of our brethrens."

"Erm, I don't mean to rile things up, but I thought Fa Zhen betrayed the Demons after having kidnapped all the children and women to force the men's surrender. Only those who ran away were spared, right?"

"That was true about the Yeo Ba and Sang Bun tribes, the real Demons your stories suggest. The E Mo tribes and many other smaller tribes were separate. We were not as gifted in battle. Chief Cao Sung inherited the Demon's strength from his Sang Bun mother. He failed to calm both sides and was ultimately forced to arms."

Elder Ci moves adjacent Bai Hu, sending a serious, steady gaze over the crowd. "The Demon Slayer, Bao Lai, has come to our aid. We owe her, in the very least, civility for the laudable rescue at Ji You. The Demon General Bai Hu from Nan Rong has also accepted her as a friend and ally, as would the great Cao Sung. If anyone here has one fraction of respect for our hero's legacy then I implore you to put differences aside."

The message is repeated a second time in the E Mo's language. Deadly eyes remain on many faces. Either respect for Cao Sung or simple group conformity ultimately draws the majority to concession. A handful leaves the building while many more move to the outskirts of the gathering to shirk from joining discussions.

"Please do not take offense, Demon Slayer." Elder Ci bows regretfully.

"Actually, I was expecting a lot more rocks thrown. Ha ha!"

"Not really the time to be joking, Wife. Even I thought that was tactless." Bai Hu swings around and pokes a heavy finger at my cheek.

"She's not your wife," Dui asserts grimly.

"She's not yours either." Hu shrugs.

In one swift sweep, Hu's big arms capture my body. A wave of gasps and murmurs break amongst the crowd. Actions speak louder than words and there's no misunderstanding this gesture in any language.

"Whoa, Bai Hu! Wh-Wh-What are you doing?"

"Make things easier for yourself. Play along." Hu whispers gently before planting a sweet peck against my cheek. He looks up to convey the message to a reaching Dui, who abruptly withdraws.

Hu's reputation as a warrior combined with his uncanny resemblance to the great E Mo hero makes a strong case. Cao Sung's approval is enough to turn a few unfriendly stares. At length, all elders, excluding Ci, make their way to the middle. Hu loyally stands guard with one arm around my shoulders. Dui takes to my exposed left.

"Enough formalities." Ci whispers the translated version to our party as an elder in crimson fur dismisses another's attempt to begin the usual ceremony. "We don't have time to spare. Another of our girl was found dead, right at our doorsteps. That leaves fifteen potential survivors and an evasive murderer. Another fruitless search. What about you?"

"Yue Na has not made any progress," a representative in light robes calls out in the E Mo tongue.

"Neither has Ming Na," Elder Ci sighs disappointedly. He immediately repeats the interjection in the other tongue. "However, Elder Gui's star reading has led us to believe the culprit is a Demon Slayer. It was by no mean coincidental that the Heavens sent us, not only a reflection of the great Cao Sung, but also a Demon Slayer of our own. We will find the party responsible and bring them to justice."

"Flowery talk! That's all that is! What benefit does any of your flowery talk provide? Five are dead! How do we find the rest before everyone else follow?" The elder in crimson glowers. Her long silver braided hair swings madly as she throws Elder Ci a hard glare, citing in her own language, a flurry of frustration, most of which resembles expletives, which the translator could not bring himself to expound.

Several more interjections ring out from every corner of the room. Each drowns beneath the next. Disagreements turn to commotions, which in turn become uproarious quarrels. Each has counter arguments to their opponents; others fuel the flame. None seems to have the answer. Above the discord, wrath from the elder in red fur dominates. Her booming voice echoes with the force of war drums. Her eyes carry daggers. Despite the vast number present, flying fury from the lady is particularly aimed at one poor soul: Elder Ci.

"Who is that woman? What is she saying?"

"Lady Sa is Er Na's chief elder," Ci whispers in return. "Er Na is not happy with us. We haven't pulled our weight in the investigation, is her contention. Ming Na suffered the most from these tragedies and has expended the least resources in searching. Fact is, while our sister cities have insisted on keeping E Mo troubles within, we've been reaching for outside help. The E Mo cannot remain isolated. Aimlessly wandering the desert will prove fruitless. You and General Hu are our best hope."

Pausing, Ci casts a troubled smile. "Is something the matter, Master Dui? You seem less convinced."

Spinning a dazed, wide-eyed stare toward Ci, Dui's jaw tightens. Slowly, an exhale escapes. "I'm merely startled by the accusation. We were sent to seek advice from whom I thought would be a level-headed woman. Lives are at stake and this pointing finger back and forth is the extent of our guidance? What else is she saying?"

"Oh, just that she's not happy outsiders were invited to this summit. Lady Sa is a firebrand elder to be sure, but she has a good heart."

"Does that mean she won't talk to us?"

"Ah... well, I think we best give her time to calm, Demon Slayer, before storming her tent for advice."

Ci's easygoing smile is met by silence. Dui falls into deep contemplation while Hu continues to watch the main foray. For a time, the interpreter looks back and forth from the general to the council and then at length, shifts his body fully toward Hu.

"Your attention has been wholly captured, General. Can you understand their bickering?"

"Not a word," Hu shrugs.

"No? I thought perhaps your resemblance to Chief Cao Sung might not be coincidental."

"I'm a Southerner through and through." Slightly puffing out his chest, Hu nods as a mean to reaffirm his allegiance. "Body language. I was looking at the council for body language. Everyone except for that loudmouth is completely oblivious or not even paying attention."

"I am truly sorry. The E Mo are usually a bit more grac—where are you going, Doctor?"

Without any notice, Dui moves through the crowded room and approaches the council, bowing to Elder Sa before joining the others on the dais. Ci nervously follows his lead.

"If no one has an idea then I have a plan." The booming, controlled, and assertive tone is uncharacteristic of him. Dui despises being the center of attention, and as I recall, public speaking is one of his worst fears. The man who has suddenly captured the room through seemingly born leadership, holds little reservation.

Ci stands a step below the dais and gives the translation as requested. Dui bows in appreciation and continues. "A trap for a trap. After all, this has been nothing more than a trap. Deceiving Governor Lu, framing the E Mo, slowly torturing only female victims, and then sending back their mutilated bodies. If it were mere vengeance against the E Mo, none would remain alive. He could have killed everyone ten times over. Instead, the E Mo have been trapped inside this invisible prison while loved ones are taken. These acts resemble incidents from Ji You. It's highly probable that the culprit pointed fingers at the E Mo as a mean of baiting another."

Steadily, Dui's direct stare cuts through the heavy crowd. "You."

"Don't you go pointing fingers at her!"

"Dui's not, Bai Hu. I... have thought something was missing from this picture too. It's as Dui said, the murderer could have killed everyone. Drawing in the Governor was unnecessary when he has no trouble dirtying his own hands. If every act until now has been pieces to a trap, then we've fallen in. Things will only escalate from here."

"I knew it! It's your fault! *It's all your fault my sister's dead!*"

The voice echoing from beyond the door is drowning in heartbreaking tears. A boy rushes inside, dagger raised, and is instantly knocked against the wall. The weapon in his small pinned hand drops from suffering the severe force of an opposing gauntlet, sending a reverberating thud throughout the frozen hall.

"Calm down, boy!"

"It's her fault! She admitted it! How can you defend that killer? She did it! *She did it!*"

"She didn't do anything wrong!" Hu scowls. Furrowed brows immediately glance over his shoulder toward the wide-eyed doctor. "What the hell are you trying to do, Dui, get her killed?!"

"Bai Hu, let him go."

"No, Bao Lai. This boy needs to shut up and listen! All of you! Bao Lai saved your ass in Ji You and she didn't have to come back to save your ass a second time! Fa Zhen, Cao Sung... they're all dead! Get over it! Whoever this bastard is, we'll find him and make him pay! Stop bickering. That's not going to get us anywhere!"

"My sister died because of her!"

"Your sister died by the hands of a murderer. Avenge her if you want, I won't stop you, but find the person responsible. Don't make a scapegoat out of Bao Lai just to feel better because you're scared."

Those were harsh words for a boy. They were also conveyed through such a fatherly tone that rage quickly subsides from the small face peering up. Lips tremble, tears well in big round eyes, and then the boy pushes away Hu's hands and runs out the door.

For a moment, Hu looks after the retreating child, troubled. There was something about that boy which was all too familiar. Lonely, confused, and lost. Those expressions were Hu's when we met two decades ago. I knew he was an orphan. That might be all I really know about his past before Tian Mao Yi.

"Hu—"

"I'm tired of this back and forth. What's your plan, Dui?" Brushing off the shadows creeping over his brows, Hu turns back to the dais.

Sighing, Dui runs a hand over tired face. "We took the bait but the killer hasn't changed his methods. The recent victim was another provocation. In any case, he's counting on Bao Lai to stand with the E Mo and oppose Governor Lu. Devastating casualties will inflict both sides. However, if we make her the solution, that might ruin his well laid plan and draw out the killer."

"And how do you propose we do that?"

"Give credit to the wrong Demon Slayer. Turn her over to the Governor and this conflict will end."

"Oh, that's your plan, sacrifice Bao Lai. Is that all? Why didn't you say so sooner? *Are you stupid?!*"

"Hu, please, give him a chance. How will that help us find the missing women, Dui?"

"This trap was meant for three: the Governor, the E Mo, and you. Peace for the E Mo won't be permitted. He'll either strike against the Governor or the E Mo to resume the conflict. We just have to be there to catch him."

"Nice plan but what about Bao Lai? He wants her dead, so how is handing her over for execution going to ruin his day?"

"As far as I'm concerned, this man wants everyone dead. The question is what do these three pieces have to do with one another? Governor Lu may know more than he leads on. Same as that grieving boy, he's looking for the quickest way to soothe his pain. If he were absolutely sure an E Mo was behind this, these cities would have been burned to the ground."

"You're going off on a tangent. Finding out who this man is, won't help us find those women. The best trackers have failed. What difference does it make once we have a name? I say we bait him with the obvious. Plant a story about Bao Lai and set up enough traps to catch the murderer. Whatever demon slaying skill he has won't work on me."

"If the killer were straightforward, we'd have faced him in Pa Xu. Mock him with a cheap trick and he'll send back another body."

"I won't sacrifice Bao Lai."

Dui doesn't have to explain, I know he'd never put me in danger. The exasperated doctor sighs and says no more. On the other hand, short-tempered Hu chains big arms around my shoulders. Hu's an intelligent and capable general who tends to become careless whenever worry gets the better of him. He's always been protective of me, ever since we were children. This time is no different.

"Listen, boys. You both make good points. So, let's do both."

"I'm not putting you in danger!"

"I'm already in danger, Bai Hu. Until we find this man, so is everyone else. The immediate thing we can do is assuage Governor Lu and rid one impasse. I agree with Dui."

"B—!"

"Bai Hu, listen to me. I agree with Dui."

Worried gold eyes peering down are so tenderly sweet that I forget to breathe. He's become even sweeter than the man who was once my *Handsome Husband Hu*.

"Please, Bai Hu. You have to understand."

All I can think to do is wrap my fingers tighter around his arms and return a hard stare. Wavering eyes narrow. For a time, it feels as though we're the only two in the room. The hard jaw clenches and I anticipate rebuff. Yet, grudgingly, Hu lets go.

"I'll do whatever you want, Bao Lai."

Elder Sa's simple acknowledgement through a nod signals concurrence. The summit continues with an air less heavy; though, also solely in the E Mo tongue. With our roles expired, Dui moves off the dais and slips out the door. Hu and I follow suit, leaving the crowded building behind.

Chapter 6 – 5

"All right. What's going on you two?"

Once we're on the desolate southeastern road toward the agricultural reservation, Hu finally breaks the uncomfortable silence. Dui, who's taken lead, turns about on a heavy sigh.

"I'm surprised by your self-control, General. The old you would have stomped your boots until things fell your way."

"Don't make me sound like a brat. Out with it. What are you trying to pull? One mention of sacrificing Bao Lai and I'll end you here and now."

"For a soldier, you're really dense. There were hundreds of people in that room. Any could have been the murderer or his friend."

"Which murder? The Governor's daughter or the E Mo women?"

"Either. We're outsiders and outsiders aren't often given the entire truth. Jumping to conclusions without proofs makes us pawns. In some ways, we already are. Let's just keep eyes and ears open until further notice."

"Dui, are you being completely honest? Is there something else we should know?" I don't want to doubt him but he seems more troubled by the earlier discussions now that we're away from the summit. Palms are closed into fists. Dui's chewing on his lips.

"You can tell me anything, you know that."

Hesitantly, the doctor looks up and down the empty road. "I... don't want to make assumptions without more proof."

"But?"

"But... this ordeal may not be as black and white as we thought, especially when our allies are purposefully misleading. Elder Sa was pointing fingers, that part was true. However, Ci's statements that Ming Na suffered most from these trials are in direct contention with Elder Sa's opinions. She claimed Ci's previous report was false, that not even one person has gone missing from Ming Na, let alone the three brought to their council's attention."

"Wait a minute. You understood what she said? When did you learn to speak E Mo?"

"During my time with them some years back. I picked up a thing or two. I've told you about my travels, haven't I? Most languages have the same basic root."

"Well, yeah but, I mean, that's really impressive."

"Big deal!" Bai Hu huffs with hands on his hips. "Ci exaggerated, so what? There's still a killer on the loose. Let's focus on that."

"Ming Na enlisted our help. Ci had no reason to lie. Also, didn't you find his fidgeting odd, General, when he thought you understood the E Mo tongue?"

"Maybe he was afraid we wouldn't sympathize. Who knows? Why? Do you think Ci is the killer? Should have called him out when you had the chance."

"I think we shouldn't jump to conclusion. And, I'd appreciate it if you'll keep silent about my... linguistic advantage."

Hu shrugs. The detached attitude suddenly overcoming the doctor puts a scowl on his counterpart. I have to concede that Ci's dishonesty was uncalled for. At the same time, believing an E Mo would do this is preposterous.

Silence creeps into our midst, and as the sun is beating down rather vigorously, I attempt to push conversations along. "Ci may be questionable. I trust Elder Gui. He thinks a Demon Slayer is behind this."

"Who knows if there is a Demon Slayer? Many of Governor Lu's men were stationed at Ji You. He might as well have been responsible for the E Mo's detention. It's not farfetched to believe someone here killed his daughter out of vengeance. Taking a life is inexcusable; though, in the E Mo's case, understandable. Their women and children were tortured and killed. What justice was there after the fact? Not one word of apology. Not one wrong has been righted. As for the women currently missing, maybe one or many from Man Wan sought retribution for Cai Yun."

"All you have are empty theories. First, Bao Lai was the target, and now, there may not be another Demon Slayer. Make up your mind. How is handing Bao Lai over to Lu going to keep her safe?"

"If there is a Demon Slayer and the first theory is right, the culprit won't let her reach Man Wan, not if she will remove pressure from the E Mo. If the second theory is right, speaking to Governor Lu might give us insight into who is behind these killings. Either way, I say we make our way to Man Wan. For now, consider Bao Lai a Southern general's lover. Diplomacy will keep her safe."

Pretending to be Hu's lover would keep me safe and yet, hearing Dui assert the idea without any reluctance, breaks a tinge of pain across my chest. This past year has not provided my heart one moment of peace. Just when I thought there was a chance to move on, the future has become out of reach.

Then again, presumption has gotten the better of me. As quickly as he said those words, Dui's calm eyes waver. I can't stand how easily he brushes me off and simultaneously suffers heartbreak. If he'd outright hate me, I could look away. This limbo of uncertainty... it's the same one in which I'd placed him.

Finally, I understand how he must have felt all this time, being in love with someone too stubborn to return that love when affection was never lacking from either side. The question then becomes which of us is more obstinate. He's forgone entertaining any further notion of romantic attachment between us. It's up to me. Either I give into Dui's distant companionship or push the doctor into falling for my whims, though the latter would prove to be a challenge. Since the day everything changed between us, he has been trapped in unending desolation. The kindest thing I can do for Dui is not the kindest act for me. Once more, selfishness has become too tempting.

Chapter 6 – 6

"Your robe's torn."

"Hmm?"

Hu's finger digs into the hole of my pink robe, onto the exposed shoulder. The same finger then pokes my cheek while he takes the seat adjacent. He's been waiting for a quiet moment together ever since Elder Ci came to brief the council's decision. Er Na and Yue Na will continue their search without influences from outsiders. Nevertheless, Dui's advice was considered reasonable and Ming Na was permitted to follow through with his plan, so long as repercussions are kept solely within Ming Na. For the council, it means safety from Governor Lu. For us, the first phase of our trap.

"Where's Dui?"

"Dui again? How about, 'Hey Hu, I'm so glad to see you're as handsome as ever!' Even a, 'How are you, Hu?' would be *greatly appreciated.*"

"Sorry."

The Demon General is pouting. I'd forgotten how adorable he can be. The mildly flushed cheeks grow pinker whenever he'd look over to the stupid grin on my face. After a while, tense shoulders slump.

"He's busy examining the dead girl's body."

"Oh. I didn't even think to do that."

"I don't blame you. It smells like hell over there. The oddball finds it all very *fascinating* though."

"Hmm, sounds about right. When it comes to scientific discovery, little can divert his attention. Guess we should leave him alone for now. By the way, thanks for saving me earlier, on all accounts."

"What am I good for if I can't protect you?"

Scanning over the pink robe, Hu frowns upon perceiving the numerous patches. Considering heavy wear and tear, even through several melees, the robe has been surprisingly durable. "I'll buy a new one for you once we're back in An."

"You're awfully confident, Xiao Meow."

"I'm hopeful and optimistic... should I feel optimistic? You'd left because I was a jerk. I'm not anymore, I swear."

"I know."

"So... does that mean you'll forgive me?"

"I've already forgiven you, though really, I owe you an apology too. I wasn't there for you when you needed me. I... ran away, basically, when things became difficult. I'm sorry."

"Nah. If I were you, I'd left me a lot sooner. Jealousy got the better of me; I wasn't the man you deserved.

Still, I've... missed you. There hasn't been a day since you left that I haven't regretted every stupid thing I've said and done. It's not too late, is it?"

Why does he keep doing this to me? Every single sweet thing out of his mouth makes me feel guilty for the elation welling inside. It's not unfaithful to consider another relationship with Hu, I know that, but the idea of being without Dui doesn't sit well with me. I can't have both. At the moment, I have neither. What I need is more time.

"Should we really discuss this now?"

"Why not? The world doesn't stop for anyone's misfortune. Misery and bloodshed are as common as day and night. There's little time for happiness. Whatever little is left, I want to spend it with you. I love you, Bao Lai."

Love. Despite the romantic in him, Hu's never before admitted that he loves me. Love to him was conveyed through physical desire. Marriage was an incredible notion he would anxiously consider only under duress. These gentle tempting and honest words, more so a genuine proposal of an everlasting bond, were ones I'd dreamt of receiving. I want to accept them, to mend this wound in my heart, but I'm afraid.

"I've made you cried again."

Soft little kisses from his warm lips whisk away the tears welling in the corners of my eyes. Those big arms

I've missed so much wrap around my back, pulling me into the painfully nostalgic embrace. These feelings for him which I've buried are slowly rising inside. I don't want to suppress them anymore. He's been honest and I want to return that honesty. If I can't be honest with him then, I can't be honest with myself.

"I love you, Bai Hu. I'll always be in love with you. Those days in An as husband and wife, however brief, were some of the best days of my life. For a time after I followed Dui to Pa Xu, those memories served as both comfort and regret. I regretted not having appreciated them more. I regretted not having made you understood how I felt. At times, I regretted leaving altogether."

Eyes widen and then immediately narrow from a broad smile. Those soft lips descend toward my own. While my body trembles from desire, a sharp pain in my chest turns an ashamed gaze downward.

"I love Dui, too. It's not right for me to accept you when I'm pining after him."

"It doesn't bother me." Hu nudges up my chin. Shaking his head gently, the idea of sharing my heart seems to have been his expectation.

"It bothers me. I just... I need to think things over. Right now, I'm afraid for you both and the E Mo. Who knows how many other lives could be drawn into this conflict? There's too much at stake."

"Excuses, excuses. Give me a little credit. Who do you think you're talking to? Twenty years ago, we couldn't keep one secret between us. Six months ago, we were lovers. I'm more than familiar with both your mind and body. Whatever's keeping you from giving a straight answer isn't fear of this conflict. Otherwise, you'd never have come."

"I... right, sorry. I'm... confused and maybe... a little... guilt-ridden right now. There's nothing you can do. I just need to work through this. Could you... please give me some time? I'm not making any promises—"

"Is that all? Yes, I know all about your guilt-prone tendencies. Must have been residual influences from those ascetic monks. Three months with them ruined you for life, huh? Glad I left temple before they came back. God, were they depressing!"

"Hu—"

"I get it, I get it. You like Dui. What else is new? Same as back then, I'm always by your side and despite what you may think, I know you're still mad at me. I'm sorry. I really am. I'll wait as long as it takes until you forgive me. That doesn't mean I'll stop trying."

In an instant, a smile appears. In the next, large palms run up the length of my waist, sending unbridled chills down my back, while a warm tongue leaves a sensual trace on my lips. It happened so fast, by the time I realize his mischief, Hu's already moved away.

"Didn't I say it's only polite when someone's kissing you, to kiss back?"

He starts up, winking impishly. I've forgotten how to breathe. If my heart won't explode, my boiling cheeks will. It's been so long since I've felt desired in such a fashion, all sorts of impure thoughts are racing.

"That's... um... terrible logic?"

"Should have known. You're still the most unromantic person in the world. Accept that as a token reminder of what you're missing, Wife." Grinning, Hu takes the road leading to the city center.

Chapter 7: Mue Ran

Sometime during his absence, Dui was able to enlist help from leaders of the other two cities, who began rumors that the culprit, a Demon Slayer, has been caught infiltrating Ming Na. The culprit was captured by Nan Rong's Demon General sent to investigate the women's disappearances by Prime Minister Zhang Tang. He's also taken it upon himself to deliver the killer directly to Man Wan for execution, thus ensuring the E Mo's safety from the Northern courts. To make things more believable, small gatherings were thrown to celebrate this good news. Doors were once again open to outsiders in hopes the killer will target the obvious: our caravan.

All night, I tossed and turned from hopeful expectation that our gambit will catch the culprit before anyone else is killed. The more I tried to calm racing thoughts, the more I couldn't stop thinking. It's nearly sunrise now. There's no point to continue struggling.

The air is freezing. The fur blanket can only do so much. My lungs are beginning to burn. As I walk toward the cultivation area, apricot-colored light sets aglow surrounding stonework. The sight is mesmerizing, though pales in comparison to another wonder not far ahead. Beneath the sheet of draping early morning light, brown hair flutters softly in the wind, as does the familiar grey and blue robe.

A year ago, I had to fight him just to detangle the fuzzy mess on that head, and lectured daily so he'd bathe at least thrice a week. We always joked about everything, all the while, I knew next to nothing about the silly man. I'm afraid now I know too much, and as a result, fallen too hard. Those days in An when he used to tease me in that lecherous fashion, I should have returned each bout in kind.

"Are you all right?"

"H-Hmph! Wha—? S-Sorry!"

How in the world did that happen? I was a ways down the road and the next thing I know, my face slammed into his back. We're in front of the cultivation area, so that means he didn't move from the spot. I have.

"Don't daydream while you walk. Remember what happened last time?"

"Yes. I ran into a horse's butt. Pffff! Ha-ha!"

Dui wouldn't let me live it down for a month after, especially since the smell didn't leave my hair for a week. He swore I was imagining things and still the doctor made all sorts of shampoos and oils to cleanse my hair until I was satisfied. Dui always humor me. That is to say, he did.

I thought we'd eventually look back on the memory and laugh. At the moment, I'm the only one laughing. His lips remain a thinned line.

"Um... Ahem. Sorry. I'll be careful. Why are you up so early? Can't sleep either?"

"I'm not tired."

His back still turned, I walk to the front of him. "Those bags under your eyes disagree."

His eyes are bloodshot. Dui hasn't been this tired since his services during the Nan Rong – Bei Ling conflict. "Does this have something to do with Er Na? Did you find any clues? I meant to ask before we left."

"Not anything in particular."

"Liar. Something's bothering you. The least you can do is trust me, Dui. We're in this together, all three of us, so if you know anything, don't keep it to yourself."

He's looked off elsewhere, as has become the usual habit whenever I'm near. The doctor chews his lips for a time, aware that I won't give him peace until his secret is shared. Despite how he feels about me, this is one of those instances feelings should be placed aside.

"Dui."

Sighing, long fingers comb through the silky brown hair. Another exhale and then he looks down. "The girl was killed with an unordinary weapon."

"How so? How unordinary?"

"Let's just say I doubt any weapons shop would carry such a ghastly thing. What worries me are the several dead young men also laid out when I went to examine her body."

"Were they murdered?"

"No—well—I wouldn't say murdered. Heart failures, all of them."

"It's not impossible for young men to suffer heart problems."

"No, not impossible. Usually not this many at one time either, not when they were as healthy as oxen."

"Did you check for toxins?"

"Yes. For the most part, I didn't find anything unusual in the blood except for excessive adrenaline, not until I examined the latest cadaver they brought in. Under his fingernails was a white powder mixed with an ashen red compound. The white powder contained traces of psilocybin. The other half has components similar to another I encountered during my time abroad. It's been too long, I can't remember what it was, and my travel journal is back in Pa Xu. I just wonder how something like that could have made it here of all places."

"Incredible! No one thought to mention the young men? Why would they have kept quiet?"

"We're here to find the missing women. They probably thought more unexplained deaths would muddle the case.   Aside that, we're outsiders. Everything is on a need-to-know basis."

"We're also trying to help. Do you think the men's deaths are connected to the missing women?"

"I don't know. Er Na's healers were casting troubled glances and mumbling secretly amongst themselves during the entire examination. I managed to catch two words: demon and god."

"Cryptic old men chatter won't help us. What about Elder Sa? Did you have a chance to speak with her?"

"No. She wasn't the best candidate to find unbiased information on this case."

"Why's that?"

"She's... well, she... Looks like we have company."

"Who? Wait, Dui! I see through you, Mister! You're not getting away! I have more questions!"

Darn it! These kids have the worst timing! Dui deftly slips past the approaching Mo Bi and into Li Li's company.   She sidles up adjacent, capturing the escaping doctor in her arms. I can't squirm past Mo Bi's puppy eyes. My blood pressure is rising again. This is not the way to start off a morning!

Chapter 7 – 2

"Godspeed, my friends. May Heaven and Chief Cao Sung watch over you."

After our return, Elder Gui conferred necessary resources to carry forth our plans. He's grown a little weaker since last I saw him. While the elder wished to see everyone off at the gates, we decided to bid farewell in his yurt.

"Thank you. With any luck, we'll meet the killer before ever reaching Man Wan. Just in case, stay vigilant, Elder."

Ropes are bound around my hands in order for the ruse to seem believable. Hu escorts me to the main gates where our caravan awaits. We aim to reach the post at Xia Pa before continuing to Man Wan.

Stationed at the front of our caravan are Hu and three warriors. Three more are posted in the rear with Dui. I'm in the middle with two others on each side. A young man, Er Wan, is to my right. He's said to be a talented tracker and one of the fastest persons in Ming Na. He will scout our surroundings from the middle for any sign of possible interception. To my left is a face I wasn't expecting.

"Um... Hello?"

"Hi! Remember me? I didn't mean to cause you trouble before. I'm really sorry!" The chipper young woman, suddenly recalling her male disguise, puts on a somber front. She's the woman who pointed out the Demon Slayer to everyone at the summit.

"I thought Er Na wanted nothing to do with outsiders."

"Er Na doesn't, but I do. I think this is the right thing. After all, we're in this together. No matter what everyone else believes, I know you saved us from Wang Liang and I want to return that favor if I can. Huh! What an incredulous stare! So you don't remember me! We were in the same cell at Ji You!"

"We were?"

"Sure! I sat on the left side of the cell, maybe that's why you didn't see me. Mo Bi and Li Li were to your right and your attention was only ever to them."

"B-But I thought only they spoke my language."

"Whose fault was that, Miss Presumptuous?" The lady sways her hips to the right, pouting, with arms crossed. Er Wan's scoff turns her pose upright. "Whoops. This cross-dressing thing is really difficult. I'm Zhang Rai, by the way, or just Rai."

"I'm Bao Lai. Nice to meet you, Rai. Say, not that I'm ungrateful, but why are you coming? This isn't a simple escort. We're bound to face danger. Plus, why are you cross-dressed?"

"*Shh*! I'll hear no more of it. The killer is after women, so excuse me for blending! Besides, we E Mo aren't foreign to danger."

"You, uh, don't seem very E Mo to me. W-What I mean is—!"

"I'm too fair-haired, is that it?" Rai giggles.

"No, I meant your eyes are very unusual. Amethyst eyes. I've never met anyone with eyes like those."

"Oh, these old things! Left over traits of a once proud race. Nowadays, we're even rarer than Demons and Demon Slayers."

"Which race would that be?"

"Some called us Empresses, and others, Temptresses. In all, we were rumored to have been born from the moon goddess, Chang'e, atop Si Sui Mountain."

"That's... very confusing."

"Aren't you honest?" Rai throws pale hands into the air toward the sun, smiling to herself as if rejuvenated from basking in the golden glow. "I'm a descendent of the Huang Nu people, to the northeast. We were known for our beauty. Some say our tribes had nothing else but women of exceptional beauty. In the old days, men of fortune and power came far and wide to beg for our company. We were queens and empresses and now, we are almost gone."

"Why's that?"

"Fear. Beauties tend to have their way. We had too much influences over men with too much power. In a way, jealousy was as potent as fear. The very thing they once sought, became the very thing they sought to destroy. As such, we've nearly been bred out of existence. For those not so lucky... to the gallows!"

The dreadful tale is enough to send a chill down anyone's spine. Rai, on the other hand, laughs gleefully at the serious tone she sardonically imposed.

"Oh, I didn't answer your curiosity, huh? I consider myself as such, but I'm not E Mo. My master died some years back; so, I ran away from my mistress. She was the jealous type, you see, like all ugly women are. Never liked me very much. The E Mo found me wandering about in the desert and took me in. Very kind people, the E Mo. I don't know what I would have done, alone as I was."

"Er... Your master?"

"Yes. He purchased me for twenty taels from my previous master. That was the most he ever paid for any servant. Said so himself."

Servant. She's mighty proud of the expensive exchange too. I'm more inclined to believe she was a slave. And yet, Rai shares her past complacently. The bright smile and cheerful eyes are similar to those a child. She must be my age, if not older. Not a fraction of time has marred her perfectly beautiful face.

"I'm sorry, Rai."

"What for? I'm free, now. The E Mo really helped me. I want to help them back and I'll do my best to protect you too."

"That's not necessary, I mean, I can take care of myself. Don't worry."

"I'm not worried because I'm going to protect you. The Huang Nu are known for two things: beauty and grace. I'm not very strong but I can hit a flying hawk between the eyes with just a pebble. Want to see?"

"Ah-ha, no thank you! I, uh, I believe you. Yikes! That's scary."

"Ha-ha! You're funny, Bao Lai. I like you! So, is it true the handsome general is yours? I'm *so* envious!"

"He's... yeah, he's mine." Dui said to keep up pretenses for my own sake. I don't distrust Rai, I just trust Dui more.

"Where did you meet?"

"At... some place down South. We've known each other since we were children."

"*That's so nice!* I want that. A bond formed in childhood becomes love in later years. Such a romantic story! Was General Hu a great catch from the very beginning? I bet he was! Tall and handsome!"

"Well actually, when Hu was younger, he was really short—"

"Ladies, *ladies, please!* My ears are burning!" Hu steps in, grinning nervously. "There's no need for jealousy. Bao Lai dug her claws into me at an early age. It's entirely her fault, I'm head over heels."

"Don't say it like that. You make me sound like a harpy!"

"What did I say that was so bad? I thought you liked birds?"

"They're not the same thing! I never intentionally *dug* anything into you or thought for a moment that I made you feel trapped!"

"When did I say I feel trapped?"

"Just now! If we hadn't met, I'm sure you'd be relieved."

"Where is that coming from? I'm trying to say I love only you. What are you yelling for?"

There's no answer for that. I don't know why I'm yelling. That's not true. I know the thing to which I'm most fallible: guilt. Maybe I feel guilty that Hu loves me too much, loved me ever since we were children, that he'll be lonely forever unless we're together. And, maybe I fear that we'll have to part because I won't leave Dui. Or am I mad because a future with Dui is farfetched and I don't honestly know if I could walk away from a disappointed Bai Hu, whom I've come to adore even more these past few days. No, maybe I don't truly know why I'm yelling. I'm still confused.

"Sorry."

Hu's big arms capture my entirety in their loving embrace. Nostalgia from his scent sends my mind into delirium. Without thinking, my hands reach to return his warmth, only to feel the rope around my wrists tighten. It's enough to return my senses. As I lean away, Hu grudgingly lets go.

"Hmm. You're both really close, huh?" Rai cuts through the awkwardness, smiling timidly. Sighing wishfully, she moves next to Er Wan. "Lucky, lucky."

Chapter 7 – 3

The road to Xia Pa, noted as Mue Ran in the E Mo's language, cuts through the Xa Xa Desert and Sim Bay Valley. This area is noticeably hotter than the road to Er Na. By noon, heat is furiously pouring down. Set before the caravan are vast, endless horizons. The path is so daunting. How anyone lives out here is beyond me.

We've been walking for a few hours and it's felt like days. The others are keeping steady pace while my numb legs are dragging against the scorched earth. I can't tell if they're actually moving anymore.

Thankfully, Warrior Ju En, who's leading the caravan, suddenly calls the pack to halt. He points to an area shaded below a large canopy of sandstone where few tools and materials have been left behind. This must be a usual rest stop.

"Are you okay? You don't look well."

In exchange for the doctor's kind concern, my legs finally fail me. Dui fervently fans my face once we settle beneath the stone shelter's protective veil. He undoes the rope bondage and then cool fingers press against my wrist. The doctor continues going through routine examination procedures. My vision's going in and out. I can't imagine he's doing much better.

"I'm fine. What about you, Dui? Stop fanning me. Fan yourself."

"Here. Li Li's tonic works wonder. Can you lift your arm?"

The container pushed against my lips pours out a soothing grassy taste. I try to grasp it but my disobedient arm drops halfway. Black specks are beginning to form in midair, obscuring the field of vision. He continues to fan while drawing open my collar.

"Hey! What do you think you're doing?"

"She's overheated. Unsteady pupils, rising heart rate, dried skin burning to the touch. Her muscles are cramped and weak. At this rate, she'll fall unconscious."

"Ah! I thought you were awkwardly waddling! Why didn't you say something, stubborn woman?!"

Hu takes the fan from Dui and fervently swats the air every which way. The doctor pulls back the collar and wipes a nice cool compress onto burning skin. Maybe this isn't the time for this but having their attention is really flattering. It's just too bad the black specks are growing in number. Everything is starting to dim.

"I'm fine... silly rabbits... Xiao Meow... kitty... Master... Hung... mad, Dui did... like... pretty birdies... "

Chapter 7 – 4

He's been running in and out of my room all day. Poor guy. I don't usually catch colds so easily, and of all days, on my birthday to boot. As if tending the clinic alone weren't enough, Dui's been checking on me every fifteen minutes. More than that, he insists we celebrate my birthday properly. That means preparing special meals, decorations, and presents. I know he purchased that dagger and embroidered holster from Xin Po's blacksmith, the ones I've been eyeing for three weeks. The doctor doesn't care for weapons. He's as averse to entering a weapons shop as I would a brothel. That couldn't have been easy for Dui. He certainly likes to spoil me and I would be lying to say that I'm against it. The constant attention, endless devotion, and frequent doting; anything for a smile or a sweet moment beside each other. This is what it must mean to feel loved.

"April eighth! April eight! It's April eight! Ouchies!"

"Are you okay? Lie down."

Dui grabs my shoulders until I've settled back onto the ground. I'd snap out of delirium into a full sitting position, bunching the cramped stomach muscles into a knot. Breathing has become a chore. A heavy pulse is throbbing in my ears. My temples are on the verge of exploding.

Without pause, I drain the remaining liquid from the container pressed against my lips before falling back to catch my breath.

"Was that Li Li's tonic?"

"Yes. Don't worry, there are two left. You'll be fine."

"I'm worried about you, Doctor."

"Why? I'm not the one with low tolerance for heat." He replaces water on the compress and then sets the wet piece onto my forehead. "I should have made sure you'd kept hydrated. Sorry."

"Stop apologizing. I know my limitations. As usual, I was careless."

"Careless or distracted?" The mumbled words were clearly intended for himself. In the shrouding silence, they couldn't have been louder.

"Distracted by wh—oh you meant Bai Hu. Ha! Jealous!"

"If you say so."

"April eighth, Master Dui. I'm bad at math but I didn't forget your birthday."

"I'm not worried about seeing April eighth right now. The sun is starting to set. We'll freeze out here unless Er Wan comes back soon."

"Isn't Er Wan... where are Hu and the others?"

"Er Wan ran back to Ming Na for help. The rest resumed Mue Ran with Zhang Rai in your position. Doubling back would throw off the ruse. If nothing else, a Southern general would have little trouble earning Governor Lu's support. The missing women are priority. Hu wanted you to know that he would have stayed but the others needed his strength. They're no match for a Demon Slayer."

"I understand. I'm glad my predicament didn't stall progress. Sorry, I'm such a pain."

"Hu knew you'd say that. He said to tell you that's what he... 'loved best about you.'" Dui looks out toward the horizon, smacking his lips in disgust for having relayed the sweet message.

Hu's amorous ways never cease to amaze me. He's usually very open about his emotions. In other words, he's very temperamental, just like me. We're two peas in a pod, Hu and I. Dui, on the other hand, is controlled. Our opposition in nature is one of the aspects which drew me to him.

"Thank you for staying with me, Dui."

"I'm a doctor. I don't have a choice."

"Meaning if you weren't a doctor, you'd have abandoned me?"

He's glowering again, except this time there's a pink hue on those cheeks. From this angle, they're starting to match the crimson sky. It's difficult to contain myself.

"Why are you laughing?"

"S-Sorry. It's just... you're blushing, Doctor."

"You're imagining things."

"If I'm delirious, then there's really no harm in keeping my observations, which otherwise would be deemed inappropriate gawking by anyone in a state more conscious to scrutiny."

I haven't seen him this adorable for quite some time. The more he becomes the center of my attention, the hotter his face grows, until even the tips of those ears are turning pink. Whenever he flusters this way, old habits are hard to suppress. I love teasing Dui. I love seeing his frown, his pout, his endearing sulking. Mainly, his smile whenever our row ends. The harder I stare, the closer he comes to bursting at the seams. Until finally...

"When is Er Wan coming back?!"

"We're in a decent spot, Doctor. It won't be that bad. There are enough materials to start a fire. If worst comes to worst, we could always repeat that night in Feng Jia and share body heat."

The glowering deepens. Despite the playful insinuation, that was one of the worst nights of my life. After having saved me from trouble, Dui was severely injured. We had no place for shelter while Feng Jia was under Bei Ling's control. I was so afraid that I'd lose him. There wasn't anything I wouldn't have traded for

129

his safety. Having him beside me now makes me feel so incredibly blessed. And yet, he doesn't seem to share my sentiment.

"Don't mock me."

"I'm not, Dui. I'm not mocking you. I haven't lied to you about my affections. I'm a bit used to tormenting you but this hasn't been some mean joke. What do I have to do for you to change your opinion of me? What do I have to say for you to give me a chance?"

"This conversation is unbecoming. We're stranded and innocent lives are at stake."

"Same as it was in Feng Jia, except I'm the one who've made an ass of myself, and now I'm a burden. I don't suppose you'd listen if I tell you to return to Ming Na."

"No."

"Didn't think so. Guess now I know how you must have felt in Feng Jia. Good thing Yu Qi found us. I was really glad we could meet your brother so that you could finally live for you. Sure, it was all in the moment, but that confession of yours really took me by surprise."

"I'm not interested in the past when the present is riddled with uncertainty. Please, let it go."

"No. The past brought us together. So did your tenacity. It really made me happy when I heard those three words from you. Remember what I said? I like you, Master Dui and—"

"Please just *stop talking!* Maybe you haven't noticed but I'm not the same person I was in Feng Jia. I've changed. Why don't you try doing the same and grow up!"

Dui just yelled at me. Dui never yells at me. Raises his voice here and there, certainly, but not this way. This isn't Dui or I'm still fast asleep. Maybe, the simple explanation is he's fed up.

"Sorry."

More awkward silence. For a moment I thought we were close to rekindling that special bond reserved for us two. He's not my lover. At the moment, I doubt he wishes to remain my friend. Somewhere along the line, he simply became my keeper. What a sad compromise.

Sometime after, Dui finally exhales. "Er Wan's coming."

Thank goodness. I'm disappointed to have this moment alone with the man I love cut short, but the repeating theme these days whenever we're together is only to grow farther apart.

Red glow from the setting sun drapes over the slender shape coming forthwith. The more he nears, the more defined his figure and steps become, even-paced and a little heavy. I've seen this type of movement before during my time in Nan Rong's services. Er Wan is lithe and light-footed. This figure is marching like a soldier.

"Dui, that's not Er Wan!"

Chapter 8: The Other Demon Slayer

"Come out, come out, wherever you are. I know you're here, little girl. The runner told me so, right before I slit his throat."

In the obscuring dark crevice, Dui grabs a hold of my shaking arms, drawing our bodies closer into one shadow. I know he saw us, this man whose voice I vaguely recognize. He was one of the guards at Ji You; though, not the one I speculated.

"Come out before I kill your friend too."

"Dui—"

"*Shh!*"

We have nowhere to run and our positions were exposed. There's no sense in hiding. Dui's racing heartbeat against my back is evidence that he's realized the same. Clashing swords is inevitable.

Our last confrontation demanded a cheap shot to disarm this man, the luxury of which is not possible in this instance. I'm not in any condition for a fair fight. All the while, Dui's mounting heartbeat is signaling consideration for a reckless gamble. I start to turn toward the doctor when, in one swift sweep, he moves into the light with a sword latched to his hip. Dui's not exactly built for combat. I didn't know he even had a weapon.

"What do you want?"

"Where's the girl?"

"Which girl?"

"Don't play dumb. Your so-called killer, the Demon Slayer. Bao Lai, was it? Champion of the Savages. Hand her over."

"She left with the caravan."

"That's not what I heard."

"Then you heard wrong. Who'd leave the prisoner behind on their way to court?"

"If she's a prisoner then you're her keeper. Why are you still around?"

"Waiting for that boy you killed. He had my supplies. I'm not made for this weather so I'm going back. You might have bested Er Wan but he's outwitted you. The caravan's long gone."

Pursing thin lips, the killer mulls over Dui's rational persuasion, while silence sweeps over their standoff. From tone to expressions to body gestures, the execution was stable and natural. Any average opponent would have fallen to Dui's quick thinking. As fate would have it, his opponent is far from average.

The doctor said to abstain from invoking my ability, but at this rate, the confrontation can't end peacefully. However, try as I might, Tian Ji Zhong Shi Yan won't surface. Yu Qi's chi technique must have permanently blocked my ability.

A swift ripple of wind brushes against the dried earth, a loud crash of metal grinding against metal, and then several more sweeps of blades cut through the air. The doctor, who once could hardly lift anything heavier than a sack of rice, is keeping pace with the killer, a former soldier of Bei Ling's army. His movements are fluid and he's doling out an equal amount of force, matching the killer swing for swing. This isn't the insecure Dui from An who belittled himself for lack of brute strength. My inappropriate swooning aside, he's grown as manly as Bai Hu, maybe in some ways, even manlier.

Those long days spent at Tian Mao Yi, I thought Dui was merely instructing apprentices. Apparently, he was also training on the fields. I'd teased him a few times for being a fragile little thing. I just never thought he'd go this far to change that perception. I wonder what else he has been hiding from me.

"This is as pointless as it gets!"

"Shut up!" Yang screams in response.

Yang was one of the soldiers stationed in Ji You during the Nan Rong – Bei Ling conflict. He nearly killed Mo Bi while his friend, Jai, targeted Li Li. I had suspected the perverse Jai as the person behind these kidnappings since he had no trouble harassing women of any age. Yang was unconscious when I'd invoked

Tian Ji Zhong Shi Yan and he wasn't interested in casually laying hands on strange women. In fact, if memory serves, he mentioned having a lover which made him abstained from joining in the other soldiers' *fun.*

"What do you want with Bao Lai?"

"Nothing worse than your device."

"Which is?"

"Same as all the savages'. It only takes a fraction of a second to kill you. I'll let you live for a fraction of the truth. Where is she?"

"Real men don't betray their allies, just as real men of honor don't resort to cheap tricks."

"Honor is useless when you're dead. Nothing but a crutch to men with something to lose. I don't have anything left. What the hell do I care?"

"So you're afraid of dying. Don't you know? Overusing your advantage will lead to your demise. An unavoidable cost of Tian Ji Zhong Shi Yan."

"I said shut up!"

Flurries of blades collide, neither having the advantage. After twenty bouts, the long-awaited opportunity finally arises. Yang's mad dash results in exchanging his position with Dui. The dagger latched around my ankle, the one Dui purchased for my birthday, flails toward Yang's back as I move out from the hiding place. My arms are still trembling from effects of heatstroke; the dagger couldn't make full impact. It was enough to draw his attention before my legs give out. Taking advantage of the opening, one strong sweep from Dui's blade and the sword in Yang's hand is lying a distance away.

In the blink of eye, Yang disappears, and in the next instant, his hand is on my throat. However, he's in more shock than I am. The fervent twitching and furious darting eyes overtaking his confused expression were mine a few moments ago. He's suddenly lost the ability to invoke Tian Ji Zhong Shi Yan. Now I know why I couldn't either.

"Do it, Dui! Do it now!" What little strength is left goes to binding Yang's arm.

In spite of his newfound warrior spirit, the doctor is hesitating. Taking a life goes against everything he believes, and while he desperately tries to find the resolve, it becomes apparent things won't end here. My weakened grips are slipping. Yang's going to kill the both of us once he manages to separate from this totem and me. It'll only take fractions of a second, far less time than I need to throw off this necklace and match his level.

"Doctor, get the potion ready! I'm going to use the skill! In case my heart goes into cardiac arrest, you know what to do!"

"Don't, Bao Lai!"

"I have to, Doctor! He's going to kill us anyway! I might as well chance Tian Ji Zhong Shi Yan. If something happens, you can save me. You're the only one who can!"

Blood drips down Yang's left shoulder onto the tremulous arm. The dagger is still lodged in his back. I'm losing my grip to his mounting retaliation. It's only a matter of time now. Dui clamps down trembling jaw to form the resolve that's ripping away at his conscience. The doctor brandishes the blade and rushes forthwith at the same time Yang successful wards off the pain from his injury for a short moment, sending a hard gauntlet across my face.

The next thing I see is twilight as my back slams against the ground. When I look up, the two men have disappeared.

Chapter 9: The Enemy of my Enemy

Elder Gui sent a small party to investigate an unexpected shift in the wind toward Xa Xa. They were too late. Er Wan's lifeless body was retrieved to Ming Na, after which, this rowdy pair snuck out while the adults were busy. Li Li came for Dui and Mo Bi, for me. I would lecture them both but I just don't have the strength. It's freezing cold. I can barely feel my feet from inside the thick hide boots. The fur blanket covering my entire body, from head to toe, is still not enough. These old bones of mine are aching from the penetrating chill. The rest of my body is recovering from heatstroke. For the time, Mo Bi's carrying me on his back.

"I can't believe you lost Master Dui!"

"I know! I'm sorry!"

Li Li's hands are on her hips, lips puckered from displeasure, as they have been for the last thirty minutes. "How could you not have seen where they went?"

"Yang used Tian Ji Zhong Shi Yan."

"Why didn't you?"

"The totem was around my neck. Direct contact nullified my advantage. Here. Keep this thing as far away from me as possible. If you can pin it on Yang, all the better."

"Did he hurt you, Miss Bao Lai?"

"Thanks for asking. I'm fine, Mo Bi. I'm really sorry about poor Er Wan. When this is over, please help me express condolences to his family."

"Er Wan didn't have any family, Miss Bao Lai. That dead girl they found in Er Na was his lover. He volunteered for the dangerous escort, knowing the stars were against his sign. Elder Gui warned him. I heard when they found his body, there was a smile on his face. The elders said the lovers are reunited."

"Whether that's true or not, he would have lived if I had taken precaution. It isn't right for innocents to suffer this way! I should have known better!"

"Maybe you fell ill because Er Wan pushed his luck." Mo Bi nods as a mean to impel a small sense of comfort.

"That's preposterous!"

"Not any more preposterous than Tian Ji Zhong Shi Yan. Hey, can we use this to find that man?" Unperturbed, Li Li swings the retrieved totem in circles from the end of the woven rope. Similar to Gui, her strong beliefs and irrefutable acceptance of fate is something to be desired. "Oh, wait, I know! Let's ask Pak Teng!"

"Who?"

"To Bi's dog. He found me once when I was separated from a hunt. He's great at tracking!"

"You just want a reason to talk to To Bi. Li Li likes him, Miss Bao Lai."

Mo Bi snickers mischievously, just as a small boot stomps hard against the ground.

"No, I don't!"

She's blushing, rather profusely. This is the Li Li I expected, the shy girl from Ji You who teetered near a protective elder brother, not the experienced woman who sultrily fondled Dui.

Strange. In half a year's span, the frail, carefree doctor turned into a serious warrior. The distant, disinterested general, who rebuffed me, has become sweet, loving, and committed. The once innocent Mo Bi and Li Li are hardly just that; the latter now my rival in love. Everyone is seemingly putting on an act. Unless Dui was right, people change and I need to grow up.

I've been too focused on what it is that I want from Dui, I've lost my reason for coming to Ming Na. We wouldn't be in this mess, Dui missing, Er Wan dead, and the elite caravan heading in the wrong direction, if I'd spent all my time finding solutions to this problem instead of goading Dui into entertaining my romantic whims. Hu's strength and Dui's intellect have been the basis for this investigation. Everything has been placed on their shoulders and I've only been adding to that burden with my head in the clouds. Had my condition not separated us from the caravan, Hu would have effortlessly done away with Yang. To top things off, it's only a matter of time until Yang realizes my bluff and dispose of the doctor.

"Mo Bi. Could you do me a favor?"

"Sure. What is it?"

"Could you put me down and follow Mue Ran to fetch Bai Hu?"

"You want me to go back?"

"Yes. Yang's injured. He won't be a threat for a while. Find Hu and tell him to come back."

"O-Okay. What about you? Can you walk?"

"I'll manage. Li Li, will To Bi let us borrow Pak Teng?"

"Sure. He's probably out hunting now."

"Good. Some of Yang's blood laced my clothes. It might be enough."

"Wait, Miss Bao Lai, I trust you and all but Li Li is..."

"I can take care of myself, Mo Bi."

"I meant you're such a brat, you'll put Miss Bao Lai in danger!"

He didn't mean that. Mo Bi's worried, as is expected of the elder sibling. Implementing an offhand insult is his way to avoid admitting that brotherly love.

"Why is it always about Miss Bao Lai? I'm going! Master Dui needs me!"

"You'll get in the way!"

"No, I won't!"

"Okay, kids. Calm down."

"*I'm not a kid!*"

Yikes! What a temperamental pair! My ears are ringing from both sides!

"Don't take my head off, you two. Youth is a compliment. You'll appreciate it when you're my age."

"Aren't you only twenty-seven?"

"H-How'd you know my age, Li Li?"

"Know thyself and know thy enemy. I won't let you win so easily, Miss Bao Lai. You can have Master Dui over my dead body!"

"That's what I said about you!"

"What about me?"

"No one likes you, Mo Bi!" The young girl pumps fists up and down.

Oh, great. Here we go. Their loud squabble is going to make me deaf. Though, in a way, I feel nostalgic. I imagine this was the same reason Master Tai Hung slapped the troublemakers upside our heads. These two, fighting like dogs and cats despite the fact that they love one another, is reminiscent of Xiao Mao and Little Hung. Same as we were, they're also easily sidetracked.

"Enough, you two. Dui and the hostages are in danger. How much farther to Ming Na?"

"S-Sorry, Miss Bao Lai. Pak Teng's not in Ming Na. To Bi's hut is on the Ji Lin Hills. That's about thirty minutes if we turn east here and take a shortcut through Hou's Tunnel."

"Wait, there are people here aside from the E Mo? Who's on Ji Lin?"

"Sure. They're nomads, mostly outcasts and remaining members of decimated tribes."

"They're also great hunters, especially To Bi." Li Li adds timidly, unaware of Mo Bi's knowing grin, which is directed at me along with a friendly nudge.

"Is he? Hunters are typically great trackers. Have the folks on Ji Lin tried finding the missing women?"

"No. The outcasts keep to themselves. Plus, our elders don't trust them." Mo Bi looks up thoughtfully through a scholarly expression most likely learned during his studies in Sai Mi. "They like to take whatever they want without permission and some of our ladies were harassed while out foraging a few years back. Then, there was that incident when soldiers from Xia Pa thought we were hiding wanted criminals from Ji Lin and our city was caught in the foray... it was a big mess.

Some elders even think they might be behind the recent murders."

"No way! To Bi would never!"

"Did I point fingers at your precious To Bi? I just told Miss Bao Lai what happened."

"Well, that's not fair! Some of their people are really nice!"

"I said 'they' and all you hear is 'To Bi!'"

"There! You did it again!"

"Did what? I didn't accuse To Bi!"

"Might as well have with that attitude!"

"All right! Geez! Calm down little ones! Beggars can't be choosers. We need all the help we can get, so why don't we let the folks on Ji Lin prove themselves, huh? The least they can do is make amends for past troubles. Come on, let's ask for Pak Teng. I'll protect Li Li. Mo Bi, could you please fetch Bai Hu?"

"Are you sure? I could carry you to Ji Lin and then find the General."

"I've rested long enough. Thank you for everything you've done."

"D-Don't be ridiculous. I asked you to come, Miss Bao Lai." Blushing, Mo Bi gently sets me down. He nervously rubs the back of his head and then swiftly turns north toward Xia Pa.

"I'll be quick. Good luck! Don't cause too much trouble, Li Li!"

"Same to you!"

Chapter 9 – 2

Holy cow! Pak Teng is as big as a cow! So big, in fact, the woolly creature lets me ride on his back while he sniffs for Yang's blood. Yang couldn't have gone far with a dagger in his back and Dui in his arms. With luck, there might be traces of blood on the ground nearby.

"Tell me again why that man took Master Dui."

"He needed medical treatment and I might have said Dui has a potion that can keep Tian Ji Zhong Shi Yan from killing him."

"Does he?"

"Not that I know. Dui's smart though. He'll come up with something to stall time."

"Hmm." Li Li kicks at a patch of low grass beneath her hide boots.

For a time after, the only noises between us are shuffling feet and Pak Teng's loud sniffs. Li Li stares off into the heavens and the horizons, quietly sighing, sending puffs of clouds into the cold air. She's sincerely worried for Dui. So am I. With each passing second, the weight on my chest is becoming heavier. If we don't find him soon, I'm going to lose my mind.

"I'm sorry." Wavering voice accompanies the odd fidgeting. Li Li kicks a few more blades of grass.

"Hmm? What for?"

"For... Ji You. I should have done the right thing. Then, this wouldn't have happened. Master Dui would be safe and those women would still be alive. Er Wan too."

"What are you talking about, Li Li? I was the one who picked a fight with Yang and Jai."

"To protect me because I hesitated."

"Are you nuts? I wouldn't have let you go with him had you begged me! No woman deserves to be treated that way; no man either! They were criminals in imperial armors! A disgrace to real soldiers! I don't know why Yang is doing this but I won't let him get away with it. Don't blame yourself. You and all the hostages never should have been taken to Ji You."

"It's just... W-Why didn't Yang just kidnap me instead? He could have just taken me from the city and... did what he had to those girls. W-Why did he spare me and kill them? Elder Gui said everything that happens is as dictated by Heaven. Life is fate but what about actions and consequences? It's not fair! Those girls didn't do anything wrong!"

"Neither did you, Li Li."

Tears bead in the corners of glistening eyes. Instantly, as they threaten to fall, Li Li turns away. Boot stomps against the cold earth become noticeably harder. Her increasing pace aims to keep ahead of Pak Teng.

Poor girl. She's put on a hard front to hide the silent torture of guilt for some time now. Li Li's right, this is unfair. To her, the victims, and the E Mo people who must face repeated injustice and persecutions for their ancestors' sins. Enough is enough.

"W-Whoa there! Pak Teng! S-Slow down! Li Li, what do I do?"

"Hmm? Huh? Just don't fall off, Miss Bao Lai!"

"What kind of advice is that?!"

The cow-sized dog suddenly takes off like the wind, leaving Li Li behind. She's running to catch up, laughing all the while, for the scared-stupid look on my face. Frightened as I am, knowing that Pak Teng has found a scent trail provides a great sense of hope.

He continues west, zigzags south, turns north, and then swerves this way and that. By the time my numb arms are on the verge of falling off, the large, shaggy creature barks a few times, wags his bushy tail, and then comes to a halt. There underneath his nose is a patch I'd know anywhere. The cute panda embroidery from my blanket, with his sulking smile, is a faint reminder of Dui.

"Miss Bao Lai! Did he find something?!"

Li Li scuttles forward. Leaning a hand on Pak Teng, she slumps over to catch her breath. Her endurance is admirable, not to mention, she's incredibly fast. The star-laced heaven above was a blur during Pak Teng's expeditious sprint.

"Are you all right, Li Li?"

"Yes. What's that?"

"Pak Teng was following Yang's blood but seems like he picked up my scent instead. This is a patch from my blanket. Dui must have dropped it."

"Aren't you a little old for something that juvenile?" Li Li points to the panda in my hand, puckering her mouth from disbelief.

"That's not the point. Dui was here. He probably ripped the blanket to bandage Yang and then left this for us to find. Yang's smart. He wouldn't let Dui leave behind any trace of his blood. This patch is easier to miss because it sort of blends in with the ground, you see."

"How does that help us, Miss Bao Lai?"

"Well, if they rested here then that closes the gap from when he took Dui to when you two came to fetch me. What I mean is they can't be that far away. Plus, Yang's injured so um..."

"You have no idea, do you, Miss Bao Lai?"

"G-Give me a break! I'm trying my best here!"

"All adults, except Master Dui, are completely useless! Here, Pak Teng, find Master Dui!"

"Er... Where did you get that?"

Pak Teng takes a heavy sniff off the sock retrieved from Li Li's knapsack. I didn't think she was that obsessive.

"Poor Master Dui was fussing over a needle to patch this hole on his sock. His time is too valuable to waste on trivial things. I offered my services. If only I hadn't washed it. Oh well, let's try anyway."

"And you just happen to carry it around at all times?"

"It's called being prepared. See? I'd make the perfect wife for Master Dui unlike another neglectful woman."

"Right... Can we please move along? Smell anything, Pak Teng?"

The woolly creature barks excitedly, runs thirty paces forward, and then makes a hard turn around the base of the ridge. Li Li's right on his tail. I'm twenty paces behind.

"Wait up! I'm old! Give me a break!"

"Eeeek!"

"Li Li? Li Li! What's happened?!"

Dragging around this fur blanket is like carrying a bear cub on my back. The moment I drop the covers and make a mad dash after the pair, a grey blur jumps around the corner excitedly and I fall on my behind from colliding headfirst into the cow-sized dog.

"*Ack*! Pak Teng! Sorry, sorry! Are you hurt? I'm so sorry! Poor puppy!"

Swinging around the corner, the young girl rocks back and forth with hands cupped behind her back. "Why are you rubbing Pak Teng's side? Did you hit your head, Miss Bao Lai?"

"Yes! My head is as hard as a rock! Is he okay?"

"He'll live, Miss Bao Lai."

The grey shaggy creature pounces about, wagging the long tail. I guess that means he forgives me. My heart finally settles from his sweet reaction but my nerves haven't.

"What were you screaming for? Nearly gave me a heart attack, kid!"

"You're twenty-seven, Miss Bao Lai." Li Li frowns. "I was just happy, that's all."

"Wh—"

He moves around the corner before I have a chance to finish. Those familiar eyes, dark hair, and tall stature; this is the moment I've been waiting for.

Chapter 9: The Enemy of my Enemy

"Get out of the way, Li Li!"

Kicking off the ground, rage propels my entirety forward to exact vengeance. Yang remains immobile, giving not the slightest notion that he would retaliate. In his stead, Pak Teng blocks the way.

"Ack! Damn it! *Not again!*"

At least I manage to hit the ground and not the poor dog this time.

"Ow."

"You're really pathetic, Miss Bao Lai."

"Hey! Respect your elder! And you! Where's Dui? If you've taken one hair off his head, I'll take yours!"

"Hmph. Big words from someone covered in dirt." Yang, nose upturned, walks back around the corner.

The fuzzy dog sniffs my messy hair while judgmental jade-colored eyes peering down are supplemented by irate grumbles under Li Li's breath. "Pathetic. *Really* pathetic."

Nothing's making any sense. Yang isn't trying to kill me. Pak Teng is defending a killer. Li Li's not the least bit alarmed by the man who nearly slew her brother. And I'm the one who's crazy. I think I'll just lie here until my real body wakes up, wherever it is.

"Can you believe her laziness, Master Dui?"

"Dui?"

The instant our gazes meet, indifferent grey eyes awkwardly turn away. Starting up, I rush toward my dearest, pausing midway when he suddenly retreats a step. Well, that was embarrassing.

"I-I'm really happy you're okay, Dui."

Quietly exhaling, Dui marches past me toward the fur cover, plopping the heavy thing over my shoulders during the return. "You shouldn't have come in your condition."

"I was worried. Plus, the kids came to help."

"I am not a kid!"

"*Okay, geez!*"

Isn't this nice? The cold doesn't bother me so much anymore now that my blood's boiling. She's purposefully taunting me, I just know it. Dui, making no attempt to shirk off Li Li's sudden embrace, continues.

"The caravan heading for Man Wan might have been compromised, along with this entire investigation. He intended to misdirect us from the beginning."

"Who? Did what? Why?"

"The temperature is only going to drop from here. Best we rest for the night and start out at daybreak. There's nothing to be done right now."

154

"Whoa, whoa, whoa! You can't just drop a piece of news like that and then tell me to sit idle! How did you even come by this information? Don't tell me from *that* guy!"

Yang's moved around the corner. He doesn't make the slightest effort to conceal his disgust. Strips of my torn grey blanket are wrapped around his arm and I imagine, also around his torso hidden beneath the armor. So, that panda wasn't left behind as a marker then. Dui just threw it away.

"He's not our enemy, Bao Lai."

"Oh? I guess you weren't there when he swung a sword at your head?"

"Yang didn't know who I was. He was trying to save you."

"Okay. Let's pretend I believe that nonsense. Are you going to deny the fact that he killed Er Wan?"

"Er Wan... couldn't have possibly lived from those injuries."

"Injuries from what? Uh. Where are you going, Li Li?"

The young girl suddenly darts back down the path, her face as pallid as the moon above. Big beads of tears are gushing down flushed cheeks. She doesn't take a second to look back.

"Mo Bi! You sent Mo Bi after the General! How could you, Miss Bao Lai?!"

"Li—!"

"There's a killer running amok. What on Earth could have provoked you to send that boy off alone in the middle of the night?" Revulsion resonates from Dui's icy tone. Everything he thinks is clearly written on the sickened expression; mainly, the presumption that I would sacrifice anything for Bai Hu.

"I didn't know—! Because you were—and I needed—! Damn it! Li Li, wait!"

Dui swiftly yanks back my collar the moment I start after the young girl. He's taken charge of the pursuit. Wagging excitedly, Pak Teng follows in tow.

"Stay with Yang! You've done enough!"

In mere moments, they've both disappeared into the distance.

Chapter 9 – 3

"Does *it* not know staring is rude or does *it* simply wishes to be really annoying?"

Stuck between guilt and disbelief, I'd waited too long to chase after the pair. There's no way I'll find them now. Merely an hour's passed and the temperature has dropped dramatically. Though we're huddled around a fire, the dense air is hard to breathe. Yang's injuries are clearly bothering him. He can't keep from shaking.

"Don't mind me. I'm just trying to figure out how *you* of all people could brainwash Dui. Claiming you're not the killer, sure, but an ally? I wasn't born yesterday."

"Who could tell by your foolish behavior? I've seen newborns with more tact."

"Oh, well, aren't we charming? Fancy meeting you here. I'd figured you and the other perverts from Ji You would still be locked away in Sai Mi's dungeon."

"I am not a pervert," he replies almost defensively.

"Right. You already have a lover. How's that going by the way? I bet you're moping out in the middle of the desert because she dumped you, right? *Ack!*"

A dagger whizzes by, barely missing my head, before lodging onto the frigid earth behind. Upon closer inspection, that's my dagger.

"What are you trying to do, Yang?!"

"Returning your dagger since your lover asked me so nicely. Oh right, he doesn't even like you. You're pathetic. Only pathetic, ugly women give chase to fleeing men. You just can't win against that girl, can you?"

He means Li Li. In Ji You, I'd volunteered to take her place as Jai's plaything, a ruse which nonetheless, was somewhat damaging to my pride. Li Li was a stick figure and I was passed over repeatedly in spite of having practically thrown myself at the insistent soldier. With a well-endowed body of her own, she's surpassed me again.

"Uh-huh. Like I said, charming. Seriously, why are you here? People only stay angry for so long. She might take you back if you apologize hard enough."

Yang's hardened countenance averts into the darkness. Silent lamentations pour from every inch of him. Sorrow mixed with regret and unexpressed grief tear at loosened composure; shoulders tremble from more than physical pain. Lips press together to keep from quivering. When they finally part, a hoarse whisper croaks between heavy breaths.

"Cai Yun's dead."

"Cai Yun is..."

Cai Yun, Governor Lu's daughter, was the poor woman slaughtered in Man Wan. Her death was the catalyst to this conflict. Though he has little regards for just about everyone, there's not one fraction of the broken man sitting across the fire which implies he could ever raise even a single finger against the woman he loves.

"Yang, I'm sorry."

"I don't need your pity, Champion of the Savages. In some ways, you are responsible for Cai Yun's death. I might just take your head after all."

"H-How am I responsible?"

"Self-righteous meddling. I didn't lay hands on those women. Because of you, everything was taken from me. My rank, my freedom, my life!"

"So... having nearly killed Mo Bi was fine?"

"I assume you mean the foolish boy who jumped in front of my sword. That was your doing. One girl was a small price to pay for everyone else's life. You should have let Jai have his way."

"What kind of a man are you, a soldier at that? What happened to protecting the innocent? I've known bandits more courteous. You might not have been involved, but standing idle while your friends took from those victims what they can never have back, doesn't make you innocent either."

Yang threatened to take my head. The sudden feral look in his eyes proves the seriousness behind those words. For a long moment, I forget to breathe, hands tight around the hilt of the dagger lest our clash from Ji You resumes. As his lips slowly press together into a line, the piercing sharp stare unravels my nerves. On impulse, I move to defend, just as the hard gaze turns to the desert.

"You women are all alike." He scoffs, cutting off my overreaction. "She said the same."

"Who—oh, you mean—I see. Wait. You talked to her after Ji You and then she was... and now you're here... Who killed Cai Yun?"

"Me."

"You? Why?"

"I wasn't there to protect her when she needed me. What kind of a man am I, indeed?" The last thought was for himself, muttered almost as though a prayer in sought of redemption.

"W-Well, you weren't there because... she didn't want to see you or were you in hiding? I heard most of the soldiers at Ji You were arrested."

"What difference does it make? I wasn't there."

"Because of me."

"Don't get defensive when I accuse you and then turn around and take the blame when I accuse me. I get tired of women who constantly play the victim."

160

"As much as I'd like to express how highly I think of you, there just aren't enough profanities in my vocabulary. Look, I want to find Cai Yun's killer too. The fact that you're here must mean you know something. So, who did it? Who killed her?"

There he goes clamming up again. I have no interest in being his friend. When our enemy is the same, the choice should be obvious. A momentary truce toward a greater goal, same as Nan Rong's alliance with Ning in the previous conflict, is the most pragmatic path.

"Geez, I know you don't like me and I don't like y—"

"An E Mo." Shaking his head, Yang blurts out the response as though having come to the same pragmatic conclusion, or perhaps, to avoid my imminent longwinded speech.

"What makes you say that? That totem they found doesn't belong to any of the E Mo."

"It belonged to Cai Yun."

"She's... E Mo?"

"Maternal grandmother. Well-guarded secret. She never intended to tell me and when she did, I didn't believe her; didn't want to believe her. The Governor's love for exotic women made him sympathetic toward savages. Beneath the diplomatic façade, he knows they were behind her murder."

"How?"

161

"Through the same observations that doctor made. Those cuts on her body were from a patterned bone blade commonly used by E Mo warriors. From his description, they're identical to wounds found on the mutilated E Mo women and also Er Wan."

"That's ridiculous! The E Mo did not kill their women! Anyone could have purchased or traded for one of those weapons. Besides, I heard the women just disappeared. That's impossible without Tian Ji Zhong Shi Yan."

"Stop being so single-minded! The E Mo were victimized; therefore, they cannot ever be at fault. Is that your logic? Everything is impossible when you're not willing to entertain anything that challenges your dead set beliefs! Ignoring the truth doesn't turn them to lies. Praising killers do not make them saints!"

"And you're so dead set on viewing the E Mo as savages, the thought of their humanity must be disturbing! Nothing else explains those women's sudden disappearances!"

"Aside from the victims having left with the killer on their own terms, you mean? Or, aside from the killer basically taking victims and then reporting them missing? Yes, Tian Ji Zhong Shi Yan is the *only* possibility. *I'm* the only possible killer. Where am I hiding the women, hmm? In my sleeves?"

"But... W-What could any E Mo gain from these odious crimes? They haven't earned sympathy from

Governor Lu. He's threatened to descend his army upon their cities. If they don't hand over an innocent man... their entire existence is at stake!"

"Nothing promotes courage more than the prospects of oblivion. Fight or die. Wasn't that the thought racing through your mind in Ji You? The E Mo have gone soft. They'll sit wherever they're placed, that's the popular belief. Apparently, not everyone in their midst agree. Not after Ji You. Once the old feud ignites, it'll be the beginning of the end."

"That doesn't make sense. It's like you said, the E Mo have gone soft. How can a handful of dissenters defeat an imperial army?"

"A handful of sheep accomplishes nothing. A handful of Demons go a long way."

"You have it all wrong. Demons from the old stories were Sang Bun and Yeo Ba. The E Mo don't have that advantage."

"Which is your Demon General? Sang Bun or Yeo Ba?"

"He's..."

Undeniably, Hu is the image of the E Mo hero, Cao Sung. It's highly likely that during Fa Zhen's eradication of the Northern barbarians, bloodlines mixed when victims fled. Still, had any E Mo carried that bloodline advantage, hostages would have been freed from Ji You without my meddling. Hu is an exception.

"Let's say you're right, some people are trying to incite a war. Why kidnap those women? That won't stop Lu's army."

"Are you willfully stupid or still in denial? Think. When did your Tian Ji Zhong Shi Yan surfaced? Mine took form when Cai Yun's bloodied corpse became the last image I will ever have of the woman I love!"

There's no way Yang could know the skill invoked when I witnessed Hu dying on Mount Chou. Dui would never betray such personal information. If what Yang claims is true, that the E Mo are sacrificing their loved ones to purposefully induce the Demon inside in order to resume the old wars, the outcome will be more devastating than imagined.

Yang's turned away to hide from the outburst. That shattered composure, which he's doing everything to keep together under hardened heart, is a sore reminder of Mount Chou. Back then, a part of me sought to kill everyone responsible for Hu's injuries, and I might have, had it not been for Dui and Lord Han Bei. With Tian Ji Zhong Shi Yan, Yang could very well have killed to his heart's content. He hasn't and now he's here trying to stop a war. I was besotted by the idea of retribution, of defending the weak, and maybe as Yang said, to take my role as 'Champion of the Savages.'

I sought to keep one innocent man from harm and yet innocence is based on action, not circumstance. At the moment, the man sitting in front of me has not been proven guilty. Dui gave Yang the benefit of the doubt. I should try to follow his example.

"How did you know I was in Ming Na? Who killed Er Wan?"

"Rumors spread fast. Rumors spread by your lover, according to him. I came to find your help, *Demon Slayer*. I figured your close connections to the E Mo would provide invaluable information, though I knew you would not listen through any method outside of force."

"Fair enough. I admit it. I'm hardheaded that way. What about Er Wan? Your theory doesn't apply in his case. His lover was one of the victims from Er Na. That would mean he was also behind this plot, which clearly, he wasn't."

"I am sorry Er Wan's lover was so popular. I imagine that boy was merely killed for being in the wrong place at the wrong time."

"Was he alive... when you found him?"

"Barely. Just enough to point toward Mue Ran when I asked for you. Er Wan was eviscerated and his throat was cut. The boy was choking on his own blood. For what it's worth, the immeasurable pain was enough to kill any man stronger. He held on for one last act of retribution. His suffering wasn't in vain. I will see to it that he is avenged."

Grimacing, he looks down in recollection of some important notion. The bloodied token retrieved from Yang's pocket dangles from the end of a woven cord. The carved white crescent stone with the small chip midway on the outer perimeter is resonating an unusual draw. Even the golden brown flower and square knots looping through the top are oddly familiar.

"Hey, wait a minute... that's mine!"

Chapter 10: Ping Jing Fa Ling

Master Tai Hung, please keep Xiao Meow, Dui, Mo Bi, Li Li, and everyone else safe. And please, show me the way. I can't tell what's right and wrong anymore. The E Mo have suffered enough. I can understand their want for vengeance but starting another war is not the answer. To stand against the uprising would mean to keep the E Mo locked inside their cage for another thousand years. The atrocities at Ji You can never be rationalized. Yet, if rumors of their collusions against the imperial court spread, Ji You might be the best they can hope for.

"What are you mouthing now? If you have something to say, then say it."

"I'm praying! Leave me alone!"

"How's that working out?"

"Shut up."

God, he's insufferable! The last time I was up this way, another agitator who goes by Captain Xian, constantly yammered in my ears. The past is repeating itself through Yang. I thought he'd be a little grateful after I kindly shared my warm blanket to keep his injuries from aching all night. For some reason, he's become resentful, and I have spent the better part of the morning listening to him prattle on about every little thing that's wrong with me. I guess I slouch too much,

167

drag my feet too often, and have gotten wide around the girth.

"Hurry up! You walk too slow!"

"Then why don't *you* walk and give me the horse! Where were you hiding him anyway? I didn't hear one peep all night."

"Try shutting your mouth once in a while. Your surroundings might be noticeable. Now, where can I find this bastard Ci?"

"Calm down, already! Dui was merely relying on a hunch. I'm pretty gullible but that theory is still hard to swallow. Plus, we don't have any proof. Elder Ci has not once advocated violence in any manner. He even kept the council at Er Na from infighting and that would have been the perfect opportunity to cast a net for his faction. He's as calm as can be and a proud promoter of peace."

"Yes, because murderers and manipulators always show their true colors. Experiencing your stupidity has taken a few years off my life. Enough talk. My sword is aching for blood. Where is he?"

"Until I've spoken to Elder Gui, nothing's going to happen. I'm leaving you in Er Na with Elder Sa. She's as hotheaded as you are. Maybe the two of you can discuss methods to soothe your aching swords."

"That means Ci isn't in Er Na. Ming Na then? Fine by me."

"Are you in any condition to walk, let alone fight a band of Demons, assuming there are any, that is? Besides, why the sudden camaraderie with Er Wan? Don't you hate every E Mo?"

"I despise all savages. The ones who killed Cai Yun and Er Wan's woman will pay for their crimes."

"That still sounds contradictory. You are... confusing, to say the least."

"Simpletons wouldn't understand. Now, hurry up before the sun moves overhead. I'm not stopping if you pass out."

"Oh, another ornery man who likes telling me what to do. I don't suppose you know Captain Xian?"

"Out of thousands of people named Xian, I must know the particular one you're referencing? My brain is shrinking from every word out of your mouth."

"Hey, wait!"

Yang kicks the steed into a short sprint. It's taking all I have to keep from losing sight of him. Maybe I was wrong. He's not like Captain Xian at all. This curmudgeon is reminiscent of Yu Qi.

Chapter 10 – 2

Another half-baked plan. I'd thought to leave Yang in Elder Sa's care but that would simply give the short-tempered man an opportunity to snoop about and cause trouble. And he would too, considering his mediocre ability to speak the E Mo's language. The average vocabulary permitted his bluff into the city and ultimately, an audience with Elder Sa. I'm covered in the blanket lest anyone remember the Demon Slayer.

They've been going back and forth for some time now through conversation purposefully initiated by Yang in the foreign tongue. Even though I can't understand a word, there's no denying Yang's obvious charm. I was worried he'd offend Elder Sa. However, the portly lady in red fur and braided silver hair, has been listening rather intently to the prattling man. She doesn't mind me one bit and this is after having ignored my greeting.

Round cheeks puff red, almost to the shade of her coat. Elder Sa lets out a sharp, piercing laugh, so contrary to her usual irate manners, the walls around seem to reverberate from shock. In exchange, Yang chuckles, smiling most handsomely.

"Pst! Yang. What's so funny?"

Eyes close and head shakes. Yang frowns when I tug at his sleeve. "You wouldn't understand."

"Huh. I'm glad you two are getting along *so well,* but I really don't have time for this. Are you going to behave while I'm away?"

"Whatever could you mean, Miss Bao Lai?" Yang smiles sweetly. The false civility is more disturbing than ever imagined.

"Listen you—"

"No, you listen." Furrowed brows direct an angry glare in my direction. Elder Sa's guttural commanding tone sets the hair on my arms on ends. The last woman to scare the life out of me with such little effort precipitated Wang Liang's fall from her office inside a brothel, and still, I'd rather be sitting through another of that dangerous woman's lectures than here, receiving the evil eye from Elder Sa. Also, I had no idea she spoke my language.

"Don't come waltzing into my city in your less than clever disguise and think the E Mo are feeble victims in need of your protection, Demon Slayer. Mr. Yang has been honest, brutally honest, and I appreciate his consideration. The E Mo have our own minds, our own laws and traditions, and the means to defend ourselves as necessary."

"You do know he's..."

Tattling *would* put me in good grace with Elder Sa; though, I don't know why that suddenly matters. However, it won't help my case. One mention of Ji You and everyone in Er Na will have his head, and also mine for having escorted Yang.

"Stop mouthing your thoughts. You may not remember me, Demon Slayer. I was also at Ji You in the cell across from yours. I recognized Mr. Yang the moment he walked in. Chief Cao Sung taught that there is always redemption. Mr. Yang cared to learn our language and our judgment. That is more than you can say."

"But... you do know Yang's intentions, right? Sure, Elder Ci made questionable claims about Ming Na's victimhood—white lies—to keep Nan Rong's support in these investigations, but he and Ming Na's council were willing to break traditions and invite imperials into their midst. Those were not the actions of guilty parties with something to hide. In my opinion, other councils could learn from *his* tolerant view."

Grimacing, the elder throws off the fur scarf, fanning herself fervently, evidently not from heat but incense. "Yue Na and Er Na are isolationists while Ming Na seeks to build bridges with outsiders. Did the worldly Ci provide that popular opinion? Look around, Demon Slayer. See with your eyes and not your ears. Which city is by far more advanced? Whose people can speak your tongue? Greet anyone on the streets outside and hear a familiar salutation. Your *open-minded* view has made us all savages."

"I—I didn't mean it like that! Elder Ci said... you weren't welcoming to foreigners... older citizens—

prejudice—intolerance—hardship... youths were... Why would he lie?"

"Indeed, why would he diminish the E Mo's merits and make our councils appear narrow-minded to impressionable youths ready to sacrifice anything for a *noble* cause? Why would he continue to portray Ming Na as the single victim in these atrocities? No one ever suspects the wounded, do they, even when those wounds were self-inflicted?"

"She's right, you know." A stuck-up tone emphasizes obnoxiously. He's mightily set upon impressing the scowling elder. "Obviously, you're just another squawking parrot spitting nonsense fed by a charlatan. How does it feel to be so stupid?"

Yang's smirking because he knows I won't swing at him, not while the portly lady sitting beside me, who clearly favors the smart-mouthed man, could snap my arm like a twig. My only choice is pretense deafness.

"Elder Sa, are you also contending Elder Ci *is* behind Cai Yun's death and the kidnappings?"

"Finding the killer is not my job. You volunteered for that heroic. My job is to keep Ming Na from falling apart. Our people are on the verge of hysteria. After the last summit, Ci's local entourage has been staging protests under Chief Cao Sung's statue."

"Protesting about what?"

"Some are against letting in outsiders. Others are angry the council is too traditional and not progressive. The rest can't say why they're malcontents. As I've said, impressionable youths. Restless, angry, and confused."

"Frightening," Yang scoffs. "There goes the theory that hardship brings maturity. I've seen the likes of these boys. Every year, a handful shows up at the recruitment office, anxious to raise swords and spill blood, the sight of which they can't handle. Most run home after the first day of regiment training. Mindless animals, really."

"That's not fair, Yang. You can't compare the E Mo's position to imperials. Even if you're right, can you blame them after everything that's happened?"

"Respect is not pity, Demon Slayer. It is understanding and acknowledgement. Many of our people have lost their ways, alienated by their obscured places in this world. War will solve nothing. The E Mo were alone and stranded. Killing everyone else will again, leave us alone and stranded. We cannot wish for acceptance from others when we cannot accept ourselves. In the past, we've chosen isolation and so we had no allies. I will not let anyone destroy the single hope bestowed upon us by the Divine through Minister Zhang Tang."

"Er... that's, uh, what I mean is... I agree that war is not the answer, but how can you blindly say that the E Mo are entirely at fault, considering Ji You?"

"Those who use the past to rationalize the present will never see a future. Ji You transpired under Wang Liang's direct orders. The Alliance put an end to Wang Liang. Our people were freed. Minister Zhang Tang has rebuilt our cities, restored our agricultural reservations, increased trades, and until we requested for withdrawal, provided for our safety. We lost many friends and through looking forward, have made many allies. The crimes at Ji You cannot be justified but the wounds from those days have been mended as best as Minister Zhang Tang could endow. These recent unspeakable evils, the lives lost, must be rectified. Equality is achieved when we hold ourselves to the same standards we hold others."

"Again, I'm not advocating violence. If the E Mo had a hand in these recent atrocities, handing the guilty party over to Governor Lu for execution seems a little *excessive*. Couldn't the culprits be redeemed under E Mo laws, the same way soldiers at Ji You were jailed under imperial law?"

"Not very bright are you? The E Mo don't tolerate traitors and killers. Their laws are stricter than our imperial laws. Handing the culprits over to Lu would be nothing short of an act of mercy." Yang nods gently with eyes closed and a hand to his chin, a rather dramatic pose contrasting his character. Evidently, his prejudice is oddly stemmed from acknowledgement and study, not ignorance, of the E Mo way.

"Oh. T-Then, what happens if those impressionable youths are behind this?"

"Let Heaven and fate decide. Those who kill loved ones to achieve power may not wish for life when power is all that remains." The lady heaves a quiet exhale, closing weary eyes during a short contemplation. "Allegiance is by choice, Demon Slayer. I see the hesitation in yours. Do as you please even if that means from this moment forward, we are adversaries. At this point, Mr. Yang's guess is as good as mine. I will follow his instinct and find the missing girls' lovers. Should they have played a hand in these atrocities, my agents will put an end to this myopic plan. Mr. Yang, an old lady's stern lecture can only do so much. Will you accompany me?"

"Yes, of course, Elder."

Yang smiles that false smile, almost victoriously. He's really good at convincing people. I might be inclined to believe him too if he weren't such a jerk to me in private. Either Dui and Elder Sa have both been fooled by Yang or I can't let go of the past. Maybe I'm justifying his present character based on Ji You without giving much thought to Cai Yun. Albeit, love can change one's perception, the loss of love is entirely another matter. When it comes down to it, truth can only be experienced firsthand.

Chapter 10 – 3

In times of uncertainty, I always looked to my master. Since his death, letters in the form of prayers have been my method of reaching him. My existence is attestation that those letters have been answered. I know he's watching over me.

For a time after leaving temple, I wasn't sure if I could survive with nothing to my name and nothing in my hands except the good luck charm given to me by the master for my eighth birthday. A shiny black stone marble laden with fine intricate carvings of a phoenix rising toward a star are detailed through slivers of gold. It's my single treasure, one I continuous grip onto for safety as though it were Master Tai Hung's hand, the very thing I'm doing now.

Elder Gui and Master Tai Hung were more than casual acquaintances. The former knew my master's family too. For that reason, I trust the old man indisputably as though he were the master, even if I still think he's full of it. It's too bad that I can't have a moment alone to discuss Yang's overreaching supposition. Another face has refused to quit my side in spite of multiple attempts at evasion. Even now, he continues to impede our stroll. Elder Ci appears his usual calm self, but this strange attachment is awfully suspicious, especially since I've entertained all his questions. On the other hand, if Ci has nothing to hide, there's no reason to avoid the subject.

"Dui was really irritated Er Wan didn't return with our supplies. We wouldn't have survived the night had it not been for the doctor's resourceful nature. I'd like to give Er Wan a piece of my mind. Where is he?"

"Haven't you heard, my child? Er Wan has passed."

"H-He did? Wh-but-how? When? I-I'm so sorry!"

Elder Gui is fraught with lamentations for poor Er Wan. Elder Ci also sighs sadly; though, his control has not diminished. The latter languidly remarks, "Er Wan's fate was indeed unfortunate."

"I don't understand. I thought the killer only targeted women. Has something happened for this sudden shift in method?"

"It's doubtful. Er Wan's lithe figure often made him easily mistaken for the fairer gender. The killer must have realized his error and made quick work to keep silence."

"That makes sense, Elder Ci. Does that mean you think Er Wan recognized the killer?"

Green eyes broadened for scarcely half a second. His short, shifting breaths would not have been otherwise noticeable had I not suspected the elder. While an elder, Ci is rather young compared to his counterparts. Barely forty in years; somewhat plain. What he lacks in appearances is made up through silent charms. His seeming disposition is gentle. The tone of his voice is inviting. Even his clothes are soft neutral shades.

There's nothing extraordinary about this person, making everything he does easily overlooked.

"Anything's possible," Ci replies calmly. "Where did you say the doctor went? He can't be the type to leave his friends behind."

"Dui ran after the caravan. Took much insistence on my part. I just figured they needed him more. About Er Wan, where was his body found?"

"Not far from the western gates. We've thoroughly combed the area. Any further searches would be wasted time. Ah, it's late. Why don't you head to the main hall for supper? Nothing's to be done on an empty stomach."

"One more question, Elder. How many women have gone missing from Ming Na?"

"Why... would you ask that?"

Ci's smooth brows slightly knit. More and more, the idea of trickery is nudging at my conscience. Should this man be as dangerous as Yang surmised, I'm on the verge of trouble. Then again, I am an excellent troublemaker.

"I'm worried. I didn't see Li Li when I came in, Mo Bi either. He usually flocks to me and I thought for sure she'd lecture me for troubling Dui. Who knew I'd actually miss the noisy pair?"

"That is curious," Elder Gui strokes the silver beard. "Where are those two? They usually come by once a day to make sure this old man is still breathing."

"That's a little rude."

"Not at all! You'd appreciate it once you're my age!"

Come to think of it, Master Tai Hung once said this also, back when he urged me to consider an arranged marriage, so that I would have someone to care for me in old age. It must have been close to ten years ago. I think we fought for a month. Had I not met Dui, my stubborn self wouldn't have known how right he was. Having someone by my side is inexplicably comforting.

"You may have a point, Elder Gui."

"Want in on a secret? Sometimes, I pretend to be dead just to watch them scream." Following the loud whisper, the old man cackles from delight. His silver beard waves back and forth from such genuine amusement that I can't keep from laughing too. The only one who's lost interest in this stroll is Elder Ci.

"Excuse us. We must tend to some things."

"What about Li Li and Mo Bi?"

"Those two are always running off. I'm sure they did not intend to be discourteous."

"But there's a killer out there. What if he has Li Li? Haven't enough women gone missing from Ming Na for us to take precaution?"

"We have not had anyone gone missing," Elder Gui looks at the stars thoughtfully. "The Heavens have truly been kind to Ming Na. May Chief Cao Sung watch over us."

"No one's gone missing from Ming Na? How curious. That's not what I heard."

Ci turns away completely to avoid my immediate dirty look. A part of me still wants to believe that he merely exaggerated to earn Nan Rong's help but there are still some things which don't add up.

"We are all E Mo," Ci interjects carefully, his back still turned. "Pain inflicted on one is pain inflicted on all. It is narrow-minded to measure suffering of one to any certain degree of others. Ming Na has been spared by luck and proximity. Therefore, it reasons the killer is likely located somewhere south."

"Don't sell yourself short, Ci." Gui cuts in. "It's all thanks to your vigilance and hard work. The patrol units you've put together have created a fortified defense."

"Which patrol units? I didn't see anyone on my way in."

"A good defense remains invisible and makes for good deterrent. Having a large number of men on patrol will accomplish nothing aside from putting this phantom murderer on guard."

That could be true if the supposed killer is incapable of waltzing in whenever he wishes through Tian Ji Zhong Shi Yan. Putting him on greater guard just means he'll more likely use his skill to bypass security. Plus, when Hu offered to set up a series of defensive measures, Ci was quick to brush aside his help. Security doesn't matter when faced with the Demon Slayer's ability, wasn't that what he said? Of course, if Ci has been lying, why fabricate merits at all?

"That is impressive. You know, I saw five other elders at council during that first gathering and so far, you're the one who seems most vested in this, Elder Ci. Aside from Elder Gui, I mean. The others didn't bother with Er Na. That was fun, getting yelled at by everyone for defending me, huh? And then I find out the women in Ming Na have all been spared through your efforts. Overachiever! I hope they pay you well!"

"Ci has always done more than expected of him. We're very proud." Gui sounds as pleased as a gushing father. The smile on his counterpart is empty.

"Surely, there must be some way to reward his merits."

"Honorable acts are rewards within themselves when they inspire others. I have little doubt that Ci will make a fine chief elder. He'll have my support at the next ascension."

"What's that?"

"The election of a new chief elder. After my resignation, all elders may support one candidate aside from his or herself during the new moon. I have a feeling the results will be unanimous."

"Really? *You're* the chief elder? So that's why you're more revered than the others! I just thought it was because you're old. What exactly is it you do anyway?"

"Ha! The last person to address me with such audacity was Mian Shi Fen. You're just like him."

"I am?"

"Hmm. He was a little brat too. It must run in the bloodline."

"What does? And who are you calling a brat, old man?!" Gosh, it's been so long since I've gotten into a spat with my old man. The nostalgia is killing me!

"A-ha! I may be an old man but there's more power in my one finger than your entire body, child. For instance, if I order Ci here to jump on one leg and bark like a dog, he must obey."

"I hope you don't intend to abuse me just to make a point, Elder." Ci smiles wryly.

"Of course not! Though, should I give the orders, you would, right?"

"Yes. That is your authority, Elder."

"Wow! You're as powerful as Emperor Cai Pai, old man! Who knew? I've underestimated you."

"The thing about power, Demon Slayer, is once it shifts hand, it might come back to bite you in the you-know-what. Best never to abuse power. If I had made Ci comply just now, what would happen after he takes my place?"

"Oh, I have a few fun suggestions for Elder Ci. Anyhow, he's right, it is getting late. I'm going to see if I can find the rowdy pair. Maybe the watchers outside know. Could you point me to one of them, Elder Ci? Finding invisible soldiers is beyond my limited tracking skill."

"For your own benefit, please stay inside. Security serves no purpose when exposed, Demon Slayer."

"Okay... Then, I guess I'll head to dinner. Are you coming, old man?"

"Elder Gui must accompany me for some unfinished business. Go on, Demon Slayer, we'll join shortly."

As if I don't know his intention to divide me from Elder Gui. Every second together is slowly chipping away at his hard mask. Speaking of chips, that reminds me.

"Wait! One last question, I promise. Elder Gui. Do you know what this is?"

Chief Bandit Wen Meng's boon, the slightly chipped crescent white stone, was said to have been pried off a Demon Slayer and can induce Tian Ji Zhong Shi Yan. It was stolen from me before Ji You by an innkeeper in Hui Fu, so I presumed. The idea that my relic was taken in Ji You by an E Mo never even crossed my mind. Maybe Yang was right. I've been blinded by bias.

"Where did you find that?" Ci's tone is as pallid as his blood-drained face. The elder swiftly reaches for the relic fixed within his gaze. However, he's too slow.

"Hold on there, Elder Ci. I found this. It's mine. Unless you know the owner, then I'd be a thief to not give it back. Any idea what this is or who owns it?"

Gui leans over to have a better look at the dangling stone, whose bloodied cord is carefully concealed inside my palm. Ci is hesitating. Claiming ownership will be nothing short of admitting to Er Wan's murder.

"Don't you have one very much like this, Ci?"

"Yes, Elder, our ancestors' treasure—Hei Se Fa Ling. I've given it to the Demon Slayer."

"Hei Se Fa Ling was paired with Bai Se Fa Ling, if I'm not mistaken. The former protects from Demon Slayers. The latter protects from Demons. You are very lucky, Demon Slayer. The Ping Jing Fa Ling Pair, crafted by An Hu, has not been united for several hundred years."

"Assuming the authenticity isn't questionable, this would be nothing short of a miracle." Ci's glowering, aching to get his hand on the stone. I can imagine why he gave me the Hei Se Fa Ling; except, that act alone was a critical mistake. The Bai Se not only protect against Demons, it can induce certain carriers of the Demon Slayer's skill to surface. If they are two halves, then it reasons the Hei Se can induce the Demon's ability within some E Mo. Instead of these senseless murders, the key to victory was in his hands all along.

"You think so, Elder Ci? I just think I'm good at finding random junk people throw away. Oh well. If you don't know the owner then, I guess it's mine."

"Greed is unbecoming. A Demon Slayer has no practical use for the Bai Se Fa Ling."

"Pretty stones are a weakness of mine, Elder Ci. You wouldn't covet pretty things from a lady, would you?"

"I... would not. Ah, actually, that necklace belongs to Er Wan if I'm not mistaken. I will be glad to return his family's treasure."

"I thought Er Wan didn't have any family. Wasn't that the reason he joined the caravan?"

"Right. Suppose I could find the owner."

"I'll hold onto it until you do. Whoever owned Bai Se Fa Ling should know it by name. All right, then. I'm hungry. I'll see you both later."

Following a short obeisance, I start for the common area, reveling in having annoyed a continually irate Ci.

He has something to do with the E Mo's troubles, that is certain. Nonetheless, Er Wan was known for his agility. Ci is visibly slow. Had they dueled, it was unlikely Ci could have killed Er Wan without consequences. There's still a missing piece to this puzzle. I have to find what it was Er Wan saw that cost his life.

Halfway down the block, the wind whisks an ominous message through a succinct whisper. They weren't far off, but when I turn back, the pair has disappeared.

"Goodbye, Demon Slayer Bao Lai. There is much left obscured which time will make clear. Don't falter. An end often precedes a new beginning. It is as Heaven ordains. The old must make room for the youths."

Chapter 11: The Emperors' Empresses

Curious. Very curious. The elders in the dining hall were speaking in hushed tones when I came in. That's not new by any means. They've been acting strange since Dui and I arrived. The troubled looks, quiet demeanor, and constant avoidance—I'd just assumed they kept from engaging us because of the language barrier or because of my blood. Since I left Ci in a troublemaking mood, thought it would be fun to disturb their peace. Whether or not the elders understood, several brows scrunched once the ascension ceremony was mentioned.

Taking all of these coincidences into consideration, I still can't grasp the entire plan. Should Ci become the new chief elder, he could order Ming Na to lead an assault against Governor Lu. Maybe that's why Ming Na has been spared. These false merits serve to secure his position. The murders and kidnappings could have served as a mean to rile the sheep and rally support for reprisal once he takes control. I could be overreaching anyhow. There is one person who may provide some insights.

Chapter 11 – 2

"Pst! Hey, old man! Are you awake? I have a few more questions before your keeper comes back."

Dim light casts shadows on the side of the tent. The flames flicker, steady, and then flutters erratically, repeating the same fashion. Bitter cold air is nipping at my nose. It's difficult to keep still. Beyond the entrance, all is silent.

"Hey, old man. Elder Gui. Are you awake? It's dangerous to leave the light on if you're not. I'm cold. Answer me in three or I'm coming in. One, two, three. *A-ha!*"

Sprawled in the middle of the floor is the genial elder with a flaccid head on extended arm. I nearly mistook the large body tucked under the fur coat for a bear. A short distance away, a neatly folded blanket is laid across the back of a tall chair. This can't be his usual sleeping position.

"Elder Gui, are you all right? You're not playing dead to scare me, are you?"

One unsatisfactory nudge is followed by a hard shove. Again, the limp body retracts to the same position. That pallid wrinkled face, the incredibly steady position managed by the wobbly old man, mostly, the faded light of life from lackluster eyes beneath wizen brows. This can't be right. He was fine a few hours ago. The spry old codger was joking about his own mortality.

"H-Hey. Old man. E-Elder Gui. K-Knock it off. Wake up. It's not funny. Wake up. Elder Gui, wake up. I need your help, old man. S-Stop messing around. Elder Gui? Didn't you hear me, I said wake up, damn it!"

The frail body is still warm. Silver hair stirs with every light whisk of wind from beyond the open tent flap. A wrinkled hand clutching the walking stick is directed at the exit. Elder Gui was on his way out to see the moon. He wanted to enjoy as many as he had left. That eerie message earlier indicated he knew better. The old man knew his time had come.

"I-It's not fair. Not again. You don't get to leave yet, I still need you! Wake up! Damn it! I said wake up! *Master Tai Hung, please wake up!*"

Chapter 11 – 3

Have to stop crying. Definitely have to stop whimpering and pull it together. Master Tai Hung's been dead for over two years. Even back then, the old man told me not to cry when the time came, same as Elder Gui's parting words to keep from faltering. Gui was a friend, but now is not the time to bawl like an infant, not in front of this group of elders, who have not shed one tear over the heartbreaking news.

Instead of lamentations, wrinkled brows have led to fists, and civil conversations have become belligerent barking. Not one word means anything to me; though, from bodily signals and intonations, it's palpable they're fighting over the ascension.

Elder Kao moves to assert contentions through another furious flurry. Once more, Ci shrugs off the attack. In her stead, Elder Jian steps forward to exchange verbal blows. The course of the room has become Ci versus everyone else.

One last tear seeps into the soaked sleeves and then trembling hands cup behind my back. This pointless squabbling needs to stop. "Excuse me. If you're arguing over the ascension, it can wait. Elder Gui's body is not even cold."

"E Mo affairs do not concern outsiders." Ci's former placid demeanor has been wholly replaced by this commanding persona. For someone who was so close

191

to the old man, was by his side moments before his passing, Ci isn't the least bit shocked.

"Suddenly, you're an advocate for isolationism, Elder Ci. What happened to reaching out for foreign opinion? From the way things are going, I'm guessing Elder Gui was your single supporter."

Smiling icily, Ci sends down a victorious glare. "Supporters, indeed! Such traditions are outdated. Obsolete. They're best used as frames of references, not in direct practice. Traditionally, we haven't faced a crisis of this magnitude without a chief elder. Things have changed. We must be open-minded to a new age; a new way. I am the new way. A fitting leader toward freedom and enlightenment."

"Wait just a minute! The ascension is through nominations, not succession!" Elder Jian snaps, shortly before reining in the outburst. He gives me an awkward glance and then looks away.

These elders *can* speak my language! They've been feigning ignorance to avoid contact. Being isolationists or otherwise, communication with outsiders is a necessity for any elder, especially since imperial laws encompass E Mo territories. I bet they're as educated as the high priests from Tian Mao Yi.

"Elder, what do you mean by succession? Is Elder Ci..."

Jian says nothing. In his stead, Ci smiles wryly.

"Couldn't you see the resemblance, Demon Slayer? No? They say good looks skip a generation. I may lack his physical advantage, but Father was always proud of me, just not enough to admit that I am his son. Being a bastard also has its benefits. For one, I don't feel obligated to follow in that coward's wayward footsteps."

"What kind of lowlife speaks poorly about his own father? Elder Gui was a good man!"

"A good man who lets his people die from unjust is a weak man revered by fools. The kindest thing a dying man could have accomplished was to hand himself over for execution and spare his people. He was scared. Scared of sacrificing himself and scared of defending his people. All the E Mo have ever done throughout our pathetic history as slaves to imperials was complained about our mistreatment, argued over philosophical right and wrong, and when subjugated, believed in the will of Heaven. The single person in our lineage with sense and courage was Chief Cao Sung. His legacy is the tradition worth upholding. He was a man worthy of respect."

"Those are dangerous words, Elder. If you're suggesting waging war against the Northern courts, don't bother. You won't win."

"I may lose myself to pride at times, Demon Slayer, but I have not lost my mind. No, I cannot win alone. There is only one man capable of standing against the imperials and he has returned to us. This time, we will not surrender."

"I hope you're not referring to Bai Hu."

"Astounding, isn't it? Just when we E Mo are again on the verge of oblivion, a man bearing a striking resemblance to Chief Cao Sung suddenly appears in our midst, fittingly dubbed the 'Demon General.' There are only so many coincidences in life. For once, Heaven has not forsaken us."

"You're crazy. Hu would never lend his strength to start another war. He's an imperial soldier. A Southern general! Nan Rong is his priority."

"Debasement of self is humiliation, not humility. The single priority for any man is his heart. Nan Rong has no consequence over the woman he loves."

I really need to keep my mouth shut. That suggestive stare and the implications behind those words are suddenly drawing attention from the other council members. They weren't fond of me to begin with, and while I wanted their amiability, this newfound interest is slightly unsettling.

"Are you threatening me?"

"That is a matter of perception. For instance, in my perception, every Demon Slayer shares a common goal: the destruction of the savages. Father was right about one thing: this all started with you. We would not be in this predicament without your interference at Ji You.

Your heroics have cost our future. Your ambition—our peace. Father was alive and well when I left this yurt. Who was it that discovered him otherwise?"

"Excuse me? I've been blamed for a lot of things in my life but murdering a defenseless old man? That's where I draw the line!"

"Then you should have no trouble waiting in gaol while we conduct a search for a cause of death."

Cause of death? The old man died because he's old... didn't he? Ci said he was a dying man. Then again, Ci said many questionable things. The crooked smirk on his thin face alludes that any innocent notion of Elder Gui's death couldn't be farther from the truth.

Every muscle on my body has tightened into knots. I would do anything to have Master Tai Hung back. This man's thrown away family for the notion of power. The unspeakable wickedness! That is a sin etched onto his soul which will never be forgiven!

"Bastard! How could you? He was your father!"

"Yes, he was. I will do him justice, Demon Slayer. If you had a hand in this, he will be avenged."

"What could I possibly gain from harming Elder Gui? You on the other hand, Elder, have already claimed his seat while it's still warm."

The disconcerting smile, cheery eyes, and deluge of confidence pouring from Ci are means to flaunt his absolute authority, which he intends to seize by force.

"In centuries past, those with Fa Zhen's lineage have gathered in the Northern courts to claim their rightful place. After all, Bei Ling is a faint remnant of the once mighty Song. Their emperors—Fa Zhen's descendants. In recent decades, his bloodline has been as rare as ours, if not rarer. Destroy the last of the savages, Demon Slayer. Bei Ling would crown you, empress."

"Aren't you overreaching, Elder? I didn't happen to drop by Ming Na on my way to claim the throne from Emperor Cai Pai."

"Days upon your arrival, Er Wan was murdered, and now my father. We had not suffered one casualty since Ji You."

"Oh please! If I'd murdered Er Wan, wouldn't your *invisible* guards have spotted me? And if I'd killed Elder Gui, why would I have called for you? Stop projecting your guilt onto me. Is anyone here really stupid enough to believe these trite accusations?"

"The better question is will anyone here defend a Demon Slayer?" Ci sends a steady gaze across the room, smiling contentedly.

"So it is unanimous. Incidentally, with two deaths on your hand, it would be poor leadership on my part to continue amnesty. Guards!"

Chapter 11: The Emperors' Empresses

In less time than I could blink, a group of tall, broad-shouldered men are suddenly inside the yurt. Their movements are nothing short of stalking shadows. Two pairs of hands have seized my arm.

"Don't bother, Demon Slayer. Try as you might, Tian Ji Zhong Shi Yan is futile. My gift to you."

This situation isn't ideal for Tian Ji Zhong Shi Yan. Thus, I hadn't contemplated using the skill. Moreover, Ci ensured that I wouldn't even have the option through Hei Se Fa Ling. As long as he doesn't know Li Li has the totem, I'll play along until opportunity arises.

"H-Hey! What are you doing? That's completely inappropriate!"

Without warning, slithery hands glide under my robe indiscriminately. The more he searches, the more agitated Ci becomes.

"Where is it?!" Ci's breathy growl is full of panic. Despite the alarm, he keeps the tone subdued and the whisper only to me.

"Where's what?"

"Bai Se Fa Ling."

"Oh, ha! I lost it. Whoopsie."

"Don't toy with me!"

"I'm not. It's like you said, what would a Demon Slayer do with Bai Se—? Hey! Stop that!"

I'd repay his groping hands with my fists if I could. They've parted the collar to my robe and descended toward my right thigh. Who knew a self-respecting elder would sink as low as the soldiers at Ji You, in front of spectators no less? There goes the naïve idea of decency!

Ci removes the dagger from the holster latched to my thigh, along with the Bai Se Fa Ling bounded around the hilt. Dried blood on the necklace cord and blade are enough to prove his case.

"We asked for help from outsiders and this is their response. Merciless tactics to divide and conquer. Now, more than ever, we must stand strong against the imperials. They will not cease until we are destroyed. These warriors around you are the legacy of our forefathers. With my leadership, we will bring back the E Mo's golden age. Stop this infighting. Our true enemies are the imperials!"

How progressive. Embracing the old wars as a mean to rile dissension while preaching tolerance at every turn to appear holier than thou. Every word out of his mouth is contradictory. He's just spouting nonsense. I can't imagine these educated men and women would be blind to such fallacies. In the end, it seems their hatreds for Fa Zhen and resentment against the Northern courts override all logic.

"Let there be no mistake, council. Our actions are just. We merely respond in kind. The imperials sent this killer into our midst. Her death will be through their exploit alone. Take her away. Execution will be at dawn."

"You can't be serious! What proof is there the blood belong Er Wan or Elder Gui?"

"A guilty conscience begs for evidence, and still, they are not in your favor, Demon Slayer."

Things are starting to come together. Dui was right. This was a trap. Ci's vision of the great Cao Sung's return could not be complete without a sacrifice. As long as Hu believes the Northern courts cause my death, he'll blindly stand with the E Mo, just as I had. Fortunately, Ci miscalculated. He never accounted for Dui. The doctor saw through impartial, unclouded eyes. I trust him to keep Bai Hu on the right path.

"My friends won't be fooled. Those women's deaths were caused by a serrated bone blade, the same ones E Mo warriors carry. The same one that killed Cai Yun! She was E Mo too! Are you proud of yourselves? Playing victims when you're the culprits? This time, you've brought destruction upon the E Mo!"

"Shut your mouth! The imperials slaughtered that mutt for a pathetic excuse to obliterate our tribes! Her blood is on their hands!" Ci's shaking fist clutches my collar until his knuckles turn white. His face, inches away, is twisted from indescribable rage, as though he'd been slapped; far more offended than when accused of killing his own father.

Mixed sentiments spiral into a tempest within the yurt. The silent council has receded from contentions mainly due dread and confusion brought on by Ci's volatile moods. Silence is as good as consent. Ci has seized complete control.

Steadily, the infuriated elder ceases grinding his jaw. Frustration is buried under that sarcastic smirk. Condescension pours from apathetic eyes. He shrugs off all annoyance. "That mind of yours is a dreadful thing, Demon Slayer. No cell can contain your poison. I would mercifully cleanse your vile soul through the purity of death, but not before my E Mo brethren finally open their eyes. Go on, take her away. At dawn, Fa Zhen will reunite with his blood."

Chapter 11 – 4

Cold, dark and smelly. This prison cell to which Ci condemned me hasn't been used in decades. Aside from holding my breath to keep from inhaling mildew, jagged ends of hair are poking my eyeballs. That was odd of him, removing my hairpins before sending me away. I thought he doesn't covet pretty things from ladies. While my hands are bound, this fidget battle against unruly follicles is futile.

All jokes aside, I'm scared. Terrified. Dread is drilling down my spine. A tingling sensation gnaws at my chest. Now and then, sharp pains well up from my belly. I'm literally shaking in my boots; though, that's partially due to the draft. Execution would be painful, I imagine, but pain isn't the most disconcerting aspect. For the first time in my life, I'm frightened by the idea of death. I'm frightened by the idea of nothingness, of emptiness. I'm frightened by the thought of thoughtlessness. The past year has been full of unexpected twists and turns, happiness and heartaches. Even so, I would do anything to keep these memories from erasure. This is what it must mean to have something to live for.

"Damn these ropes!" One free hand and I could pick the lock on that door in ten seconds! Why was it necessary to bind my wrists? Is Ci that intimidated by me? I bet he's planning to make a show of my execution come sunrise so that no one suspects him for Elder Gui's death. Then again, I'm not thinking clearly. It's just like me to jump to conclusions and end up falling on my face, same as my confession to Dui, same as my abandonment of Bai Hu. I assumed the latter didn't care and assumed the former indisputably would.

Ugh. Now's not the time for my love life. I just need to take a deep breath and think this over. I need to approach this with logic and impartiality, as Dui would. Elder Ci is an oddball and a liar but he's not particularly strong or clever. His primary talent is to appear benign, which adds to his charm by implying a level of trustworthiness in his character.

When accused of Cai Yun's murder, his rage was, by all means, genuine compared to any other emotion he's exhibited. If it were merely an act, it only made him appear more of a madman. He really does believe the *imperials* used Cai Yun as an excuse to attack the E Mo. Never once did he blame Governor Lu for killing his own daughter. His mind's not completely gone. As for Elder Gui, the old man's time was near. There were no physical wounds. At least from what I could tell, his death appeared natural. Maybe Elder Gui's passing was a coincidence.

Finally, I'd wondered why Mo Bi was permitted to send for me when the majority of the council must have been less than receptive to the idea. Ci exploited Hu's summon and Mo Bi's request. That still doesn't explain how he knew about my previous relationship with Bai Hu.

"Oh, well. It doesn't really matter at this rate. Hey, old man—Elder Gui—if you're floating around still, can you let me out? It's creepy in here. N-Not that I'm scared of the dark or anything! Okay... maybe a little."

Silence. More unbearable silence. I expected nothing less while hoping for something more. Talking aloud makes the darkened room seems less deserted. Back when I first settled in the abandoned house near Kou after the seniors ejected me from temple, talking to myself helped eased the frightful nights. It's become a bad habit, same as mouthing my thoughts.

"No? Figures. Assuming I don't join you soon, could you tell Master Tai Hung, when you see him, I said, 'Hello' and also... 'I'm sorry?' Or, maybe just tell him that I love him and I didn't mean to give him all those grey hairs. Hmm... Elder Gui, earlier when you said the old must make room for the youths, did you really mean Ci? I understand he's your son. That doesn't make him most qualified to lead the E Mo... does it? I grasp the basis for his ambition. He does, in some crazy fashion, have a point, but I mean, he's kind of... are you even there? Hello?"

"Hello."

"*Ahhh!* I-I-I mean, w-who's there?! Never mind, who cares! I'm over here! Can you let me out?"

"Eww! It stinks in here!"

Inching right and then left, a dark shadow flitters across the room like a stalking specter, until hovering squarely in front of the cell door. A familiar click follows soon after.

"Ta-da! Am I good or what? Almost as easy as hitting a flying hawk right between the eyes."

"Erm... Rai?"

"You seriously couldn't tell from my graceful gliding gait? Shame, shame, Bao Lai."

Snickering quietly, she moves to cut the rope binding my hands and feet. Then, same as before, the graceful Rai floats back toward the entrance. To our luck, not a single guard is stationed out front. The city is eerily quiet apart from the gentle rustling of wind against tall yurts, lulling those who dwell inside into deeper slumber. This might be the last night their sleep will go undisturbed. Come dawn break, all the ugliness hidden by the veil of self-righteous shadows will be cast aside by the light of truth. I hope then, that I will not be the one standing in those shadows.

Chapter 11 – 5

The pale moon over Mue Ran dims, obscured by rogue clouds without regards for her age or beauty. By the time we escaped on two horses, it's past midnight. The exact time is elusive. When surrounded by vast endless skies, time suddenly appear meaningless. In this moment, I am alive. A certainty which continues with every passing breath.

Puffs of wind rise and fall, giving new sensation to life; each moment in stride. The situation calls for haste and yet, existing pensively in the future subtracts from the present. In the present, paths spreading forth from this point are limitless. Anything is permitted. I finally understand Elder Gui's view, I think. Above, the Heavens see all paths. All exists in tandem. All is finite and yet, nothing is, until an instance of discovery. In one of these paths before me lies the truth.

"Spacing out again. Are you tired?"

"Huh? Oh, no. This should be far enough. Thank you, Rai. I don't know what I'd have done without you."

"I said I'd protect you, didn't I?"

"You sure did. I guess that makes us even now. For Ji You, I mean."

"Do you really think I'm that petty? I didn't run back all this way just to pay off a debt."

"Right. Sorry. Actually, where are the others?"

"There were some troubles with the horses and the handsome general was worrying himself sick over you. So, I *volunteered*. Do note the sarcasm. He practically begged me. Good thing he did."

"Really? Poor Bai Hu."

"Don't worry. You lovebirds will be reunited in no time. I'll take you to Man Wan, safe and sound."

"Why Man Wan?"

"What? Don't you want to see your lover?"

That can't be right. I sent Mo Bi after the caravan before it could have reached Xia Pa. Li Li and Dui ran after Mo Bi. They would have reported Er Wan's murder and persuaded Hu to quit the course to Man Wan. Besides, Rai said the caravan's horses ran into trouble, which means Hu was further delayed. How could she have missed all three on her way back to Ming Na, especially with the giant Pak Teng following Li Li?

"Bao Lai?"

"Hmm? O-Oh, of course I do."

"Really, Bao Lai! Who wanders the desert daydreaming? Were you thinking about Bai Hu?"

"Yes and Dui too. I'm worried. Have you seen him? He ran after the caravan after treating my heatstroke."

"I did. Surprised me terribly! I thought with the General away, that gentleman's façade would have come right off! Don't look so shocked. Anyone could see the torture in Doctor Dui. His worship is nigh quixotic. I wish someone would suffer that much for love of me!"

"That's not exactly a noble wish, is it?"

"Only an unromantic person would overlook the nobility of torture. It's not how severe a man desires that shows his love and devotion, it's how severe he suffers. Any fool can love. Only a true lover grieves." Rai smiles wishfully at the stars, almost heartbreakingly, as though sending a secret message to another under a different sky. When she looks down, the smile brightens, as does hidden pain. "Well, let's hurry. Tonight's not as cold as usual. We should make good time."

"Wait. Elder Ci put me in that cell. I aim to pay him back. He's the one behind these murders. We have to do something."

"He is? I just thought you must have slighted the council. They are a bunch of stiffs. Hmm. All the more reason to reach Man Wan. Governor Lu can claim his killer. The E Mo will be saved!"

"It's not that simple. We can't let him kill any more of the missing women."

"Don't overcomplicate things. It is that simple. He'll use them to negotiate for his own safety. Now, let's go."

"Rai, hold on. I don't feel right leaving things this way. Find Bai Hu and the others. Tell them what I've told you. I'm going to seek help from Er Na."

"Elder Sa won't help you, Bao Lai. She's not fond of imperials. Wouldn't be a stretch to say she hates each with a passion. You're better off convincing Governor Lu. After all, you're somewhat of a celebrity in the Northern courts."

"I am?"

"Sure. The first female Demon Slayer to effectively wield Tian Ji Zhong Shi Yan in over five hundred years. Savior of the Demons at Ji You. Veteran of the Nan Rong – Bei Ling conflict. A few of your accomplishments. I'm almost jealous of the accolade."

"Um. This... reverence is all news to me. If my name carries such weight, Lu shouldn't have trouble sending reinforcements. I've a friend in Er Na. We'll stop Ci before he goes any farther."

"I wouldn't do that, Bao Lai!" Her horse jostles quickly to block mine from turning. Rai's head shakes disapprovingly; the frown is one of concern. "She'll throw you in jail and then what will you do?"

"You're worrying way too much. I don't mean to brag, but um, as long as my hands are free, no jail can hold me."

Rai frowns at the opposing grin, pouts, and then rolls her eyes. "And how do you intend to pick locks without your hairpins?"

"I... How did you know I can pick locks with hairpins?"

Amethyst eyes widen for an instant before a sweet smile immediately takes over. She sticks out her tongue in the same moment a light finger taps my head. "Duh! You're a resourceful woman, silly!"

A shielding smile followed by empty praises makes for basic speech diversion. Works wonders for beauties caught fibbing, according to Ma Tai Tou. However, a simple question shouldn't warrant a lie. She could have assumed any number of methods from my brutish claim. Instead, Rai jumped to the single conclusion which explains Ci's reason for taking my hairpins, despite the fact that he couldn't have known I can pick locks. The only E Mo aware of my hidden talent are Mo Bi and Li Li, along with anyone in that cell in Ji You who could speak my language.

"Say, Rai. How did you know I was in Ming Na's detention?"

"The guards told me."

"They didn't wonder why you'd left the caravan?"

"I'm from Er Na, remember? Ming Na's guards thought I was just another civilian. Come on then. If your interrogation's done, we should go."

With Ming Na on the verge of war, Ci's guards wouldn't have been as accommodating as to point out the location of the hostage slated for execution to an unrecognized woman. Furthermore, no one was guarding the cell when we came outside even though Ci made certain to bind my appendages so tightly that the ropes left marks. Why would he assure I couldn't move from the spot and yet, also ensured an opened escape route?

"Are you coming?"

"Rai, are you—What's that smell? Is that smoke?"

A faint trickle taints the night air, growing more vivid through bursts of sweeping wind. The path leading back is dark. The night is silent. Still, a sensation of disquiet is flooding the atmosphere.

"It's coming from Ming Na!"

"Lack of sleep has finally caused an onset case of paranoia. You're imagining things, Bao Lai. It's probably the usual bonfires from the outcasts on Ji Lin Hills. Come on. A few hours' ride and then we can sleep."

Rai's mare trots forward, calling me along. She's really adamant to reach Man Wan, that is to say, she's adamant that I accompany her. From this point of view, Man Wan can only mean death. Ci's plan was to pin my murder on the imperials in order for Bai Hu to lead the E Mo as the returned Cao Sung. No one would believe his nonsense with my blood spilled in Ming Na. Every peculiarity since my arrest has led to this point. I finally realize what Er Wan saw.

"Hurry now. Dawdle and I'll steal your lonely lovers. Don't blame me when I do. It's in my blood, you know. The Huang Nu are famed temptresses." Curved lips arch upward teasingly. As blithe as her words are, the tone carries an unusual hint of contempt. Even then, she's still sublimely lovely; a natural result of her blood.

"Temptresses. The Huang Nu were also called Empresses, weren't they, Rai, because men of power sought their company?"

"What of it?"

"Elder Ci claimed Bei Ling's emperors descend from Fa Zhen's bloodline. A Huang Nu and a Demon Slayer would be a perfect match. An empress for an emperor."

"What's your point?"

"I was half right and so was Yang. We were both blinded by prejudice. Each presumed a single scapegoat, completely missing the idea of perpetrators, especially a coalition between a Demon and a Demon Slayer. Elder Gui said through Fa Zhen, I will find his blood. He was talking about you, the other Demon Slayer. You stole my Bai Se Fa Ling in Ji You. Er Wan took it from you during the scuffle. Yes, I see it all now. You were supposed to frame Lu for my murder in Man Wan but things don't usually go as planned, do they? So you came back to report my delay to Ci and receive new instructions. Er Wan caught you away from the main caravan when he went to retrieve Dui's supplies. Is that why he had to die?"

"You're pointing a lot of fingers without an awful lot of proof."

"Dui is my proof. I know he's not in Man Wan and I know now, what would have happened if I had made it. What I don't understand is why you're doing this. The same blade that killed Er Wan took Cai Yun's life. The same blade that took those innocent women's lives. Er Wan fell to your blade, then so did Cai Yun. What do you have to gain?"

"I really don't know what you're talking about."

"The frightening truth is that you do. Ci's method to protect the E Mo is outlandish to say the least. Even then, I still believe he's doing this for them, and if he cares that much, he never would have brought danger to their door. Killing Cai Yun was out of the question. He didn't do it. He did, however, permitted other innocent deaths in his quest to retaliate against the Northern courts who pinned her murder on the E Mo. For an elder to trust an imperial to the point of plotting murders truly prove the power within your bloodline. By your account, the Huang Nu were abused and exploited. Instead of finding justice you just turned around and did the same to the E Mo."

A morbid scowl floods her pretty face. Instantly, a red stream drips down my cheek. Clatter from a stone landing onto the ground behind sends a frigid echo into the air. She didn't use Tian Ji Zhong Shi Yan. With her impressive skills, she hardly need to.

"Keep talking and the next one goes in your eye!" For a moment, ugliness behind beauty rears its head, only to once more be hidden by a grinning mask to which Rai grew accustomed. Her smile is friendly, as usual. The lady places one hand on her hip while the other sends a graceful wave into the air.

"Hmph. Who are you to lecture me about abuse and exploitation? There's not a target on your back. Amethyst eyes! Such pretty *amethyst eyes*, they always tell me. The common trait for a modern Huang Nu whore! What good is beauty on commoners? What good is power that can't be used? Fa Zhen's blood is my own and it's given me nothing in turn! To hell with your Bai Se Fa Ling!"

The bloodied cord slams against the ground in the space dividing us. Bai Se Fa Ling glistens in the light of the waning moon, same as Rai's irises, which suddenly exude a faint golden glow; proof of her Demon Slayer blood. Despite her lineage, the prized totem was worthless in her hands.

"Rai, I... don't know your life—"

"That's right! You don't! So shut your patronizing mouth!"

"I may not know your life but I know Er Wan didn't deserve to die. The E Mo are good people who gave you a home. Isn't that what you said? What have they done to warrant your ungrateful vengeance?"

"I'm just bored." Shrugging, both slender arms stretch into the air. She smiles complacently, all the while, hiding every fraction of former rage under the pristine mask. The notions of truths and lies meld perfectly in her demeanor so that every lie out of her mouth is markedly held as truth by none other than the lady herself.

"You were imprisoned for months on end in Ji You. Was the last conflict not enough? Must you resolve to sate boredom through starting a war?"

"Ha! What a sheltered, naïve fool of a woman. The war hasn't stopped since commencement. Imperials seek to cleanse the world of savages and savages seek to enslave the imperials, as always. The temporary truce was merely to retreat and lick their wounds. In the new age, morality keeps the imperials at bay. They only kill when execution is justified, in other words, an excuse. The savages have kept their hands steady from the overwhelming probability of defeat. Given a boost in strength, they'll be quick to lose their docent ways. Cao Sung will accomplish that."

"What about the missing women? Where are they?"

A cutesy grin, a quick shrug, and then Rai delicately stares at the sky. "Dead."

"Not all of them."

"All soon enough."

"Why? They haven't done anything wrong!"

"Neither did the Huang Nu. Such is life."

"You—! Stop using your ancestors' suffering to justify your actions! You had a life in Er Na. That is something you have forfeited by choice! Tell me where they are!"

"An Empress contentedly living amongst savages? *Preposterous!*"

Smirking haughtily, the lady jumps from the horse and removes a leather wrapped object latched to the saddle. Once drawn, the vicious saw-toothed blade is almost half a jawbone of some nasty beast. Intimidation is half the battle and Rai has the advantage. Just the sight of the ghastly thing is enough to rattle my nerves.

"Go on, use Tian Ji Zhong Shi Yan. The Huang Nu blood isn't without benefit. For one, I can easily see through your trickery."

Dismounting, I cautiously reach out for Bai Se Fa Ling. The stone glistens when dusted against the pink robe, as if happy to be treated with more dignity. In Ji You, when I desperately needed this totem, Rai had taken it from my possession. She wished to abandon her dominant Huang Nu blood for Fa Zhen's even if that meant sacrificing E Mo lives. Her attitude from Ji You hasn't changed and neither has her self-serving lies. If she could see through Tian Ji Zhong Shi Yan then there's little need for Bai Se Fa Ling, especially when gifted with such great agility, which I suspect is the Huang Nu's true bloodline advantage.

Rai urging me to induce Tian Ji Zhong Shi Yan can only mean one of two things. Either she believe the talent will kill me or she's certain I can't use it. Little does she know, I no longer carry Hei Se Fa Ling.

"Last and only warning, Rai. Tell me where the women are. Admit your treachery and make amends to the E Mo and Governor Lu. I will ask for leniency."

"No thanks." Leisurely, a delicate hand reaches into the breast pocket for a small wrapper. The dull paper unfurls to a foreign substance which she inhales in one sniff. Traces of white and ashen red powder stain her philtrum. There's victory in that condescending expression before this battle even begin.

"The Northern courts turned their backs to my lord the moment Sai Mi was seized. The E Mo are vermin in need of eradication. With any luck, they'll rip each other's heart out. Master Wang Liang would be pleased."

"Wang L—?!"

Chapter 11 – 6

Clang!

A loud echo is followed by a sharp thud. A throwing knife is lying a distance away, repelled by the glimmering steel blade. Undoubtedly, that would have been a fatal blow had it not been for my unexpected hero.

Despite his gallantry, the hero is near defeat. The stench of blood is unmistakable. He keeps a hand over his mouth to keep blood from gushing. Tian Ji Zhong Shi Yan has taken its toll; though, saving me wasn't the cause. There are other wounds dripping red streams down the soaked armor.

"Yang!"

"Go. She's... mine. I'll... avenge... Cai Yun."

"You need medical treatment! I'll—"

"Another one?! Just how many men do you have?!" Scrunching her face and stomping her feet, Rai jumps in place pumping balled fists. The pretty lady is now an exemplary child in tantrum.

"Sa's... dead."

"What...? Elder Sa is..."

"Don't ignore me!"

Immediately, Yang disappears. Five knives scatter in mid air around me, Rai's sole target, and then a loud thud hits the ground. Yang's tremors have grown worse. His heart is beating furiously and his breathing is ragged. The trembling man is practically gasping for air. Time is against him and I... can't save him. If only Dui were here. Dui could at least ease his pain. Dui can do everything I can't! He told me to stay with Yang and I didn't listen! It didn't have to come to this!

"Yang! Yang, hold on! Here, open your mouth!"

As crazy as it is, soon as the bitter mixture hits Yang's tongue, shock from the disgusting taste of mashed willow momentarily stalls his tremors. Carrying willow is a habit of Dui's and also a habit of mine. It's not much, but it's all I can do for Yang.

"Look at me! Deep breaths! You have to calm that breathing! One... and two. Inhale... and exhale. Again. That's it. Keep going. You're strong, Yang! Just hang on—*Gah*!"

"Did you forget about me again? I could have killed you a hundred times by now." Sighing exasperatedly, she gives not one thought to the knife lodged in my arm. "Man Wan. Hmm. If it weren't for that troublesome doctor and his sleuthing, I would have eviscerated and dumped your corpse in Man Wan. Tsk! Oh well. Guess I'll pin your murder on that imperial instead!"

"Bah!" In the blink of an eye, the taste of dirt from Mue Ran is no longer a curiosity. Yang tugs on my collar just as two trajectories whizz by, taking a few strands of hair. I thought by now she would have expensed all those knives.

I can't permit this to continue and yet, Dui's warning is tugging at my heart. He came a long way to ensure my safety. Invoking Tian Ji Zhong Shi Yan after all this time is no different from jumping off a ledge. After realizing I have something to live for, I've learned to fear heights.

"Y-Yang, what are you doing? Stay down!"

"Not... your... fight."

The obstinate man violently trembles while his beaten body pushes off the ground. His sword digs into the earth for support. He's barely able to lift one knee.

Yang's right. This hasn't been my fight. The moment Rai's involvement became clear, I should have sent her reeling to the ground. Instead, I've resorted to letting an injured man on the verge of death become my shield. No, this hasn't been my fight but it should have been. Love made Dui strong, gave Hu composure, and turned me into a coward. Ironically, neither Dui nor Hu would ever love a coward.

"I thought you looked familiar! That soldier from Ji You with the ugly friend!" The sharp, chirrupy voice is a dagger to the ears. Rai brings a finger against her chin, smiling thoughtfully while peering dreamingly at the tremulous Yang. "Don't tell me you're helping these savages because that rich mutt was your woman! How sweet! What a lucky girl! Had I known, I would have slit her vocal cords first and then had more fun."

Rai's sadistic smile widens from Yang's madden grunts. He's too exhausted to speak. In exchange, the enraged man tries to lunge and instead falls into my arms. Rai looks on, twirling her hair like an innocent child in one hand and brandishing the jagged blade in the other.

"Stop it, Yang! You can barely breathe!"

Gah-urrrkhm!

A low growl, resonating eerily like that of a stalking beast, disrupts the atmosphere. Yang and I stare at one another before turning to Rai. She's toggling in place as if standing on hot coals. Amethyst eyes dart about furiously and then, without pause, an indescribable ferocity overtakes the former bewildered expression. When the bestial stare land upon us, the cherry mouth twists into a grin. Her head tilts to one side.

"It's about damn time!"

Instantly, the lady disappears. On impulse, I reach for Yang's blade. From the dark furrowed brows, Yang's petrified expression along with everything else around has suddenly become silent. All, except for my rapidly beating heart. My instinct must have subconsciously triggered Tian Ji Zhong Shi Yan. Either that or Bai Se Fa Ling isn't giving me a choice.

Quickly stumbling across the field to disarm the motionless Rai, the world around nearly falls apart when her jagged blade comes crashing down. We're separated by an arm's length. My blade barely blocked the fatal blow. I thought Tian Ji Zhong Shi Yan dispersed under my control, until reeling to recover from the impact, only to find Yang still frozen.

"What the hell, Rai? I thought you couldn't use Tian Ji Zhong Shi Yan!"

Aside from the incessant cackling, there is no answer. A crazed look laces her face as she swings the oversized weapon without pause, nearly foaming at the mouth. I would be losing my ground if her aim hadn't become random. Not to mention, she seems slower somehow compared to the agile warrior from a few moments ago. If she can't use Tian Ji Zhong Shi Yan then that would explain the differences in speed, meaning she's breached my advantage through some other method. Whatever it is have made Rai lose her mind. She's following my movements and yet also swinging wildly at phantoms. Despite her poor accuracy, I can't get close at this rate.

If I break from Tian Ji Zhong Shi Yan, she'll kill Yang and me. All the while, I can't keep this up much longer. Numbing pain is beginning to spread across my chest. I need to end this before falling from cardiac arrest. By the look of things, Rai's not doing much better. Sweat is beading across her brows and the grin on her face has become a grimace. Power doesn't come without a price.

Rai's paying for hers as we speak. She'll likely fall before me but I need her alive in order to end this senseless feud between Governor Lu and the E Mo.

Think, Bao Lai! Think! What would the clever doctor do?

Rai's faster than I am. In this berserker state, she's stronger too. Even if I manage to close in, a fistfight won't fall to my favor. Disabling her massive sword would be a pointless gamble.

"Zhang Rai! Stop it or you're going to die!"

The lady's hand stalls. The dazed expression remains. Bai Hu exhibited the same odd behavior in Sai Mi during his bloodlust state when a piece of memory was restored. Acknowledging her own name must have done the trick. It's still not enough. In the hazy circumstance, fearful eyes dart about like those of a lost child, until finding the familiar dangling white stone strapped around my wrist. Bai Se Fa Ling, which has been hers longer than it has been mine, provides a single source of comfort. She's searching for withdrawal from psychosis. I may know just the thing.

"Do you want this, Zhang Rai? Bai Se Fa Ling sure is pretty, isn't it? Powerful too! I bet if I give it to Master Wang Liang, he'll surely fall in love with me. I'll become the new Huang Nu empress of Bei Ling!"

Me and my big mouth! I'd barely finish the sentence and the madwoman's already lunged, taking a few strands of hair with the frightfully large blade. There goes the theory that familiarity would restore her senses. She's become more bestial.

Time for my backup plan: run for dear life!

On the ground ahead, three throwing knives lie at the southeastern corner of the road. I purposefully let the braided cord slip between my fingers. Instead of jumping for the totem as I'd hope she would, Rai dashes across the piece as though it were another pebble.

"H-Hey, don't you want Bai Se Fa Ling? Rai! Zhang Rai!"

The low growl becomes a spine-chilling howl. Wang Liang means more to her than any precious treasure. After all, everything she has accomplished was to avenge that lunatic. To defend his twisted legacy, she willingly forfeited sanity.

Sight of the three daggers comes and goes. Unable to retrieve them with Rai stumbling in tow, my entire design's come undone. The pain in my chest is growing worse. Seems silly to think I ever worried about dying, when in a few minutes, the end will be unavoidable. Whatever happens, the least I can do is not go down without a fight.

Warm streams stain the pink robe crimson. The dagger lodged in my arm is ripped out. Rai's too close behind. I don't have time to turn and retaliate. Instead, I throw the dagger several feet ahead so that the blade digs into the ground. The instant I come up, jump over the jutting hilt, and then shortly after, a distorted gasp resounds from behind. Rai tripped over the weapon, nearly falling on her face. Using the opportunity, I turn back and bring down Yang's sword.

"Ngh!"

Thunderous cracking resonate in the still air. Losing her balance did nothing to stall her speed. A few teeth from Rai's jagged weapon are lying on the ground, along with half of the blade from my broken sword. Bewildered eyes suddenly dance, entranced by the fresh stream of blood flowing down my right arm where the tip of her blade connected. The frenzied woman swings down. I stumble back, falling on my backside, barely able to avoid the fatal blow. The giant blade immediately sweeps from the left. I lie flat on the ground to avoid the dangerous path and throw the broken weapon at her leg. Though I intended for the blade to connect, the hilt spins and lands a heavy blow against her shinbone.

Flustered, confused, and agitated, the giant weapon drops from unsteady grip. At once, three knives penetrate Rai's hand and leg. Yang's unexpected battle cries drown out Rai's bestial howls. She struggles to grasp the jagged sword but can't clasp her injured right hand.

Upon perceiving two opponents charging at once, Rai attempts to flee and falls flat on her face in the process. Glimmering in the moonlight, two of the knives are wedged in her left thigh.

Chapter 11 – 7

"Yang, I have to go back. She shouldn't be a problem anymore. Try not to kill her while I'm away, okay?"

The weary man gives half a nod, closes his eyes, and then takes a deep inhale. I'm amazed by his willpower. Ignoring the immeasurable strain on his heart from repeatedly inducing Tian Ji Zhong Shi Yan, blood lost alone from other injuries would have killed a man less stubborn.

A distance away, Rai is unconscious and tightly bound. Whatever it was she used to enhance her abilities, the cost would have been her life had she continued. Her heart rate was extraneous and her organs were overheated. Falling unconscious and losing the battle was to her benefit. At least her condition is steady. I hope she stays that way until Dui returns; otherwise, the Huang Nu bloodline will move one step closer to extinction.

"I'll come back soon, hopefully. I'm taking all her weapons with me just in case she wakes up. In the meantime, just rest. Try not to move. You've stopped bleeding but those wounds are temperamental. One wrong wiggle and you might bleed out. Got it? Don't roll your eyes at me! Look, I'm not an ingrate so... thanks for saving me. You're... not... *that* bad."

Behind the empty glare, Yang remains silent. There's much he wishes to say though I'm sure nothing nice. We're not friends by any means. For now, I'm glad we're allies. Life is humorously unpredictable at times.

"Hey."

The soft utterance is hoarse and scarcely audible. I turn back from mounting the saddle to find the weary man staring wistfully at the Heavens. The expression is gentler than I've ever expected from him. It's easy to imagine whom he sees in the stars.

"Do you... think... Cai Yun's... forgiven me?"

A difficult question. I never knew Cai Yun. Although, I suppose there is something we have in common, indelible love for strong, hotheaded men in sought of absolution. I know which answer would be mine. Upon looking to the Heavens, I can see hers. Twinkling stars have moved from behind dark clouds. There's indescribable gentleness to them, reflecting Yang's loving sentiment.

"Yeah. I think Cai Yun's forgiven you, Yang. I really do."

Chapter 12: The Elders' Resolves

Every gallop closer to Ming Na turns the faint trickling scent of smoke more acrid. Black billowing clouds cover the skies as if to spare the Heavens from witnessing the earthly inferno. Ming Na is lit crimson. An ominous beacon in the dark landscapes.

After advancing a distance more, the horse jerks back. I nearly fall from releasing the reins to cover my face. Scorched flesh, blood, and gore. The echoes of screams and clashing blades, of lives being robbed from those living and dead, resound like a hellish confession. I had hoped the previous conflict taught everyone to abstain from these horrid acts. In reality, atrocities will never cease. Until everyone can stop rationalizing the present with the past, there is no future. Elder Sa's dead for trying to build that future. We might have disagreed on some things but I, too, wish to see that future.

"Wh-Whoa there! Calm down!"

Both forelegs thrust into the air. The rearing beast is neighing as wildly as his brethren from beyond Ming Na's city walls. They've given warnings to stay away. He's merely taking heed.

"Come on! Just a bit farther and then I'll let you go. I won't have the strength to do anything else if I have to run all the way to the gates. Do me a favor. Please! Just halfway would be plenty."

Still adamant, the creature whips around. I can't force him back. Had I not tired my heart from fending off Rai, running the substantial distance from here to the gates would have been an option. The thought of facing more warriors in her league who can override my bloodline advantage is unsettling. A part of me wants to run away too. Who am I kidding? I wanted to flee the moment I started down this road. Maybe I should...

"Coward! Your friends are inside! How can you live with yourself if you won't even try?! They would never abandon you! *Don't you dare run away!*"

That's odd. I swear the horse groaned from annoyance when I yelled at myself. The creature suddenly stops fidgeting, pauses a short moment, shakes his head from side to side as if working up the nerves, and then obediently trots toward Ming Na.

By the time the western gates become visibly clear, I can't tell whose tremors have grown worse, the horse's or mine. The stench of smoke has grown so thick, it's hard to breathe. Flames crackle from every corner of the city, consuming all in their path of destruction, drowning only under morbid screams and shouts. Gates on the southern and western end have been torn down. Outside, bodies litter the ground, from old to young, men to women and children. Their last moments were spent shielding one another.

No one who survives this night will ever forget these inerasable sins. Ideological correctness. Right and wrong. Every innocent life fallen is a failure upon the human race. Blood and flesh are seared into scorched earth. Ash covers the air, each silver sliver a tear for those departed. Even then, there aren't enough to express the unspoken sorrow. For now, a silent prayer is all that I can offer until the safety of those still alive are secured.

"Hi-yah! Just a little more!"

The beast, neighing wildly, makes a brazen dash at lightning speed. The flames before us burn brighter; the heat pouring forth, a furnace. We're almost there. Come what may, this is the end.

Chapter 12 – 2

"H-Huh? What the—! W-Whoa! Stop, horsey! Ack, not again!"

Woof! Woof! Pak Teng shakes the shaggy fur excitedly, jostling three children and two seniors on his back. The cow-sized dog pounces from the thick smoke pouring out the western gates, barely stopping in time to avoid collision with my skidding steed. Following Pak Teng are Li Li and Mo Bi helping a few injured while simultaneously leading a group of women and children who have miraculously been spared. Behind them is another carrying an injured boy in one arm and a sword in the other. Blood laces his clothes. Soot covers his face. And what a wondrous face to behold! The sight makes my heart leaps into my throat.

"Dui!"

When he looks over, I'm already next to Pak Teng. The creature calls his followers forward through steady barks. He takes north toward a small advancing group in the distance, visible only through the flames of their torches. They're derived in the direction of Ji Lin Hills.

"Li Li! Mo Bi! Are you both all right?"

"We're fine, Miss Bao Lai." Mo Bi calls back indifferently.

"Good, let me h—"

"You're bleeding."

"Eh-huh?"

The firm grip around my arm is also slightly tremulous. Dui's brows furrow into deep knots over the red stains on the former pink sleeve.

"I'm fine, Dui. Are you okay? When did you come back? I didn't see the caravan on Mue Ran. Hold on, where's that boy you were carrying?"

"Ran off after his sister. It's a long story. For now, go with them to Ji Lin."

"Aren't there more people inside? This can't be everyone left!"

"That's it. Another group escaped a while ago. Those who can fight are still clashing swords inside. Go on. The others are waiting."

"No. I'm going in."

"The battle's decided. There's nothing else to be done. Goodbye, Bao Lai."

Dui turns back as if refusing to hear anymore. No matter how hard he tries to conceal those injuries, he's limping to keep pressure off the right ankle. If there's nothing left to do, then there's no reason for a man who can barely walk straight to brandish a sword. He came to Ming Na because of me, and through my obstinacy, is walking to his death.

"Wait just a minute, Dui! You've been brushing me off long enough and I've had it! Hu's in there! I can hear him! The Demon General should have easily ended things by now. He's having trouble, isn't he? I'm not leaving either of you. You've gotten stronger, I know that, but I don't need you protecting me like I'm some damsel in distress!"

"We don't have time for this."

"You're right. We don't but we may never have another chance, so... I'm sorry. That's all I really wanted to say."

That dubious stare will be the last thing I remember from Dui. He's frozen in time, same as the surrounding flames. Tian Ji Zhong Shi Yan was invoked without a second thought. I don't need a thought to save Dui and Bai Hu.

All this time, I've been secretly afraid of using this gift from Fa Zhen because the prospect of dying was frightening. The moment I saw his face, every ounce of fear shed from my soul. Dui gives me courage to move forward. Dui's given me courage to do many things I wouldn't dare dream. Leaving An to start a new life was a bold step in another direction. I'd like to think I have grown as a person these past six months, if marginally. Dui inspired that in me. Even when he was weak, he was never a coward. He's stubborn as a mule and always follows through his convictions. He never abandons anyone in need. And, in spite of the distant attitude at times, Dui's the kindest person I know. I am sorry that I've hurt someone so important to me.   That really was all I had to say.

Chapter 12 – 3

Past the guest tent, centered common area, and several sectioned living quarters, the remnants of Elder Gui's former yurt juts pathetically in the midst of the massive gathering of bodies littered abound. They must have come for guidance and refuge from the chief elder. His son gave clemency to no one. Near the deceased civilians, warriors and many elders were lost in the throng of chaos. Most are from Ming Na, others are clearly from Er Na and Yue Na. Elder Sa's forces must have collided with Ci's Demons, men whom he'd recruited from all three cities under the notion of restoring justice and glory.

Chief Bandit Wen Meng once said that Demons from the old bloodline were powerful but often lost themselves during battle, slaying friends and foes alike, and thus killed themselves from grief in the aftermath. That history is repeating itself. The ones left standing now are sorrowful, twisted creatures. Whatever has given them power has taken away their souls. There's nothing left in their expression except misery and rage.

"Bai Hu!" As I run to find him, Hu comes to find me. Same as Sai Mi, only he is able to overcome my Tian Ji Zhong Shi Yan. Everyone else and everything else is seemingly frozen in time.

Before I have the chance to continue, everything goes dark when big arms wrap around my shoulders, cradling me against his chest. Hu's nostalgic scent and protective embrace bring undeniable comfort. This feeling of familiarity and security is everything I've come to expect. If it were six months ago, I'd never leave these arms. Time has moved forward since then, despite my unwilling regrets. For now, Dui's warning is ringing in my ears: we don't have time.

Momentarily, the Demon General hesitates, until duty calls him to abstain. I look up to find worried eyes peering down from a face that's been dear to me for so long. He's covered in blood. There are several obvious wounds throughout his body; none seems severe. So long as he's alive and well, I can't ask for more.

"Bai Hu, I'm so happy you're safe!"

"Wouldn't have been for much longer if you hadn't saved my ass again. These so-called *Demons* are giving me a hell of a time! Relentless bastards have gone berserk, swinging at anything that moves, including each other. I... don't want to kill them but they're not giving me much of a choice."

That must be why he's injured. The Demon General who stormed Sai Mi didn't stay his hand for anyone and as a result, no one could touch him. This general has been fighting a losing battle to keep Ci's Demons at bay without taking any lives while civilians flee. Against his efforts, injuring these men won't keep them from cannibalizing the E Mo. The moment they took Ci's poison was the moment their fates were sealed.

"Bai Hu, don't hold back anymore. These men are bound to die soon from organ failure, just like those cadavers Dui examined in Er Na. Psilocybin and that other mystery compound are wreaking havoc on their systems."

"Dui did what? Which cadavers?"

"Oh-um-I don't have time to explain. Just do what you can to knock them unconscious. It may be their only chance. If worse comes to worse, spare them an agonizing death and a guilty conscience. Hurry. Rai broke through Tian Ji Zhong Shi Yan. They might do the same."

He's hesitating. Bai Hu's kind heart desperately seeks to protect the E Mo, as he would for anyone in need. However, staying our hands will be the death of them all. For a time, troubled eyes dart back and forth searching for resolve, until a stifled deep breath marks acknowledgement of futility. The general returns a firm nod.

Chapter 12 – 4

With everything frozen in place, I can't tell if these blows are effective enough to collapse the men. Thus, I'm also throwing their weapons into the fires. Hu, clearly displeased, follows suit. Disarming other warriors in this way seems a cheap trick, a stain on his honor, but also the most pragmatic method.

From one to the next, we make our way through Ming Na until the northern council building becomes visible. Hu's been keeping a close eye on me. As usual, I can't hide much from him. The scuttle with Zhang Rai strained my heart drastically. My chest is burning. An inexplicable chill is spreading in tandem. My breathing is growing shorter and tremors have started to surface. Stagnant flames nearby flitter once or twice before returning to their petrified states. We're in a shifting still portrait on the verge of coming to life.

"Bao Lai. Turn things back. I'll... handle the rest."

Hu's accepted staining his hands red to keep me safe. I can't accept burdening him with such guilt for a lifetime. Looking back, there were paths I could have taken to bar this massacre. I never should have gone to Elder Sa, let sympathy for the E Mo blind all logic, or spent too much time earlier subduing Rai. If I'd come back to Ming Na sooner, this clash could have ended before it began. Everything is clear in hindsight but looking back is all I can do from the present. Nothing will change. That goes for everything else in life. There are only paths ahead. In this path with Bai Hu, I refuse to let him down as I have every other time before.

"I can keep things up a bit longer. Don't stop now."

"I don't want you to kill yourself!"

"Do I look suicidal? Go on. I promise I'm a-okay!"

Snarling under his breath, Hu moves to disarm another, forcing himself expeditiously through the petrified maze. I wish I could help more but tremors have started down my tingling left arm. As long as his back is turned, I think I'll lean down to catch my breath.

"Bao Lai! Are you all right?!"

"Huh? Hu, look out!"

Sharp grinding metals echo an unearthly clash. One second later and Hu's arm would have been on the ground. Despite the narrow escape, he's given no quarter. One by one, berserkers continue to wake from the stagnant scene. Hu swings furiously to keep them at bay. My ability has dampened his advantage tremendously.

"Bao Lai, stop casting Tian Ji Zhong Shi Yan!"

"I know you're weakened but so are they. Their fake Demon abilities are diminished in this state. I won't let you fight alone. "

Hu doesn't have a moment to contend and neither have I another moment for persuasion. Clashing swords ring loudly, followed intermittently by groans of defeat. I'm in no condition to subdue these aggressors through strength. As a result, I've resolved to play decoy and draw the crowd apart while Hu flanks the men in pursuit, slamming them unconscious.

Years ago, we practiced this easy lure technique on the training fields at Tian Mao Yi under Master Zhuang's guidance. I made Hu play the decoy because he was shorter and weaker. Most of the time, we merely fought each other over nothing until field practices ended. Things have drastically changed but memories from those days will always be with me. I'm grateful our paths crossed in life.

"Bao Lai, get down!"

"Hmphf!"

What the hell am I doing? Running about with my head in the clouds almost cost me my head!

A gust of wind blasts against my left temple following a flicker of silver. Hu's blade parried the assaulter's just in time. I don't understand. The warriors in pursuit were substantially behind. They couldn't have gained that much distance in fractions of a second unless... the still-life world is moving again. Tian Ji Zhong Shi Yan lost hold. Ci's Demons have regained their advantage.

"Run! Bao Lai, run away!"

Hoards of opponents gather. Some from the other areas we thought were cleared. With each encroaching foe, his attention becomes more divided. Still, Hu continues turning back to watch over me. Multitudes of wounds are adding to his battered body. He won't let them kill me but he's also hopeful he can save them. Hu's doing everything he can to keep the berserkers from advancing. His good nature is working against the futile ambition. At this point, the course of this battle has become painfully obvious: it's them or me.

I want to run away. I'm screaming at myself to run away but my body has apparently defected to another's control. An icy hand has reached out and enveloped all of me. Blood is pumping at lightning speed. My whole body is throbbing. The veins in my head are on the verge of exploding. All my limbs have gone numb.

"Bai Hu. I... can't. I'm... sorry."

Chapter 12 – 5

Everything is spinning. In the dizzying haze, a surging wave boils up my throat and then a ball of blood splatters across the ground. Half of my vision has gone dark and the other half is beginning to fade.

"Bao Lai! Bao Lai, don't go!"

Someone's muffled voice is filling my ears with desperate pleas. The echoing whispers are fraught with such heartache that I feel my own tearing apart. It hurts too much. I want to sleep but this phantom won't yield. Neither will the strong pair of arms allow me to fall from their embrace. Sharp pressure circles my chest. Slowly, echoing muffles grow hollow. Distant voices are beginning to clear.

"Is she alive?!"

"Yes! Barely!"

"Take her out of here!"

"She's not stable enough to move. The shock could kill her!"

"Damn it! Isn't there anything else you can do?"

"I— Ngh!"

"What's happening? What the hell's going on, Dui?!"

"Elder, put down your weapon!"

"Don't bother reasoning with that crazy bastard! He's the one person you're allowed to kill! Protect Bao Lai at all cost!"

"That goes without saying!"

Bleary dark sky and smoldering blaze are all I can vaguely distinguish through unsteady vision. Blood curdling howls, exasperated groans, and heavy thuds saturate the empty air between reverberations of clashing weapons, which increase in tempo as if fueling the flames.

One heavy blow is ensued by a shout. Ci's victorious cackling and the scent of fresh blood pervades every dulled senses. Dui's startling groans suddenly shift the hazy world into clear view. Blood's trickling down the doctor's right sleeve. The broken sword in his hand is all that's left from colliding with the powerful Ci, whose superficial strength has taken away the last of reason.

Having witnessed the ill effects, the elder still chose to take the drug. Just as Elder Sa declared, those who kill loved ones to achieve power may not wish for life when power is all that remains. Ci finally has control over his beloved Ming Na, a now burning ghost town fraught with death. The drug was merely used for a coward's escape. He relinquished memories for a chance at peaceful death. Yet, as wide as the eerie smile is on his twisted face, tears are pouring down those pale cheeks.

Brandishing the cold steel, Ci charges wildly. Whichever swing he cannot parry or evade, Dui's body shifts to redirect the fatal blows. Blood stains his shirt crimson. Even if he would run away, the injury on his leg wouldn't take him far.

I know he won't run. Dui would never leave me and neither will Bai Hu. There's something wrong with the latter too. He's much stronger than this. Fake Demons are powerful but compared to an original, the battle should have ended long ago. Hu could easily cut through their weapons and send the men into reeling darkness. He's fighting as a soldier and not the Demon General. Maybe, he can't.

Damn it! Tian Ji Zhong Shi Yan is our last resort and I can't cast it either. My body feels like lead. Aside from blinking, nothing else will move... except for my big mouth.

"H-H-Hey..." Ugh, dried blood tastes worse going down than coming up. "Yuck. H-Hey! Elder Ci! Is this what your father would have wanted?"

Stiff shoulders momentarily jerk back. He stalls from confusion and just as quickly, shirks off the fraction of guilt permeating into what little conscience remains.

"Bao Lai, be quiet! You're making him angry!"

Dui's not exaggerating. The elder is swinging more wildly, though same as Rai, his aim is becoming terrible.

Chapter 12: The Elders' Resolves

"Elder Gui was really proud of you. He was ready to place Ming Na in your hands and this is how you've repaid his trust? Was it worth it to kill your own father? I'm surprised a spineless coward like you could carry out the deed. I know you thought the imperials placed Cai Yun's murder on the E Mo, so they could eradicate your tribes, but it was Zhang Rai who killed her and the other girls. Did she kill Elder Gui too? Did she give you the drugs? You knew she was a Demon Slayer and still trusted her despite your prejudice. Was it hard to say no to a beautiful woman who promised you the world? She was ever just another of Wang Liang's pawns who played you for a fool."

"Shut... up!" Ci swings around, sword clenched so tightly, his knuckles turn white. A faint glow breaks across furious eyes, crimson in hue, in place of the Demon Slayers' gold. The change couldn't sustain.

Glad to know I can still get on his nerves even when he's not in his right mind. This was about as far ahead as I thought. My half-baked plan doesn't solve anything aside from giving Dui a short moment to breathe. Hu can't hold for much longer. It's a miracle he's lasted this long.

Ci sees through the diversion. Ignoring the invalid, he makes for the person who poses the greatest challenge. Dui moves to cover Hu's back, simply to have the enraged elder knock him aside from one sword sweep, cutting through Dui's already whittled blade.

"Bai Hu, look out!"

Phwump!

Hu's helmet jostles as he rolls aside to evade a collapsing opponent to his front, an act that incidentally saves his head from Ci's flailing blade. Right at the elder's feet, one Demon after another slump onto the ground until no more than half the number remains. Soul-wrenching howls break the cold morning air as the long arms of death come to collect dues. The fallen men furiously scratch at their chests and bellies, and when no satisfaction can be found, ram heavy fists against hearts and heads. Blood bursts from every orifice. Bellies boil and bubble from overheated organs resulting in all bodily functions ceasing at once. Their deaths are painful. Dying for the sake of a fool's ambition is the greater punishment marked on their souls. Sorrow floods eyes staring into the abyss. In their last moments, I pray they've found salvation.

"No..." Ci's breathless whisper carries grieving distress, not that of a madman, but one whose mind has come to terms with lucidity. The nightmare of destruction which he tried to spare the E Mo at all cost has come to fruition by his own hands.

Shoulders tremble uncontrollably. Eyes widen from disbelief, spinning wildly in search of freedom from conscience. In their course, pure hatred spreads over his expressions the instant they find me. Satisfaction turns grimace into a smile. He's found a scapegoat to relinquish frustration and guilt. He has another chance to take my head.

246

"Bao Lai!"

"Dui, stay back!"

"Don't hurt Master Dui!"

Blood. All I see is blood. In a blur, the world shifted during some precise moment when time stood still. It must have. Blood covers the ground where Ci once stood; his sword in pieces. The remaining men in front of Bai Hu have been knocked back by an indiscernible yet powerful unseen force, rendering all unconscious.

Dui shakily lifts off my body which he instinctively shielded through his own. After staring at one another wordlessly for some time, we still cannot believe the turn of event. A distance away, the snarling red-eyed Demon looks about aimlessly, purely bewildered, more so than her spectators. Once that wandering stare encounters Dui's steady gaze, the Demon's red eyes slowly begin to fade, and rosy cheeks take their place.

"Oops." Pigtails swings timidly as Li Li slowly rocks back and forth from embarrassment, chuckling innocently as though having accidentally knocked over a vase.

Moments later, shuffling feet of a protective elder brother follows suit, calling for her retreat. He meant to keep her from trouble but Li Li was right all along. She can take care of herself and... she does have me beat in every aspect. I ran into a burning city to save Dui and Bai Hu, and nearly died in the process. Then, I needed them to protect me. She managed to save us all without batting an eye.

I think I'll just close my eyes for a while.

Chapter 13: Dawn of a New Age

"Mphmf! Blargh!"

Why does my mouth taste like blood and willow? What on Earth happened? Why am I lying on the ground looking at the clouds? Why can't I move my body? Wasn't I just running on the fields with Bai Hu? That can't be. Bai Hu left Tian Mao Yi.

"Stop mouthing your thoughts and rest."

A groan turns into a whimper. There must be an invisible boulder set atop my chest. I can't turn my body to find the person lecturing me; though, I would know that voice anywhere.

"Dui."

"Yes?"

"Is Hu okay?"

"He was just here. Your eyes were open. Don't you remember?"

"I... don't know. Where did he go?"

"Hu and the rest of the caravan set off to detain the unconscious berserkers."

"The caravan's still alive?"

"Yes. They ran off when the odds were against their favor. Discretion was the better part of valor, so they said, until conscience called them back. Just so you know, a while ago, some of Lu's watchers conveniently came for a report. Expect an interrogation. They could have called for reinforcements sooner, those good-for-nothing."

"Oh. Is everything over now?"

"Yes, it's over."

"Thank goodness. In case they interrogate you first, tell Governor Lu that Zhang Rai and Elder Ci were behind the murders. Zhang Rai is Wang Liang's agent; though, I'm sure she acted through personal volition. The E Mo didn't know."

"That's neither my obligation nor yours."

"Huh?"

"It's time the E Mo stand together and meet the imperials as equals. They will never earn respect with Zhang Tang as their single advocate or the South as their mouthpieces. Pak Teng found the missing women, three are still alive. Their stories will shed light to wrongdoings from both sides. The Northern court is finally ready to listen. The age of speaking through the sword is over. I hope that given the opportunity, the E Mo will not hold back their voice. Ci sought to do the right thing through the wrong method. However, there was reason behind motivation and that reason is the objective they must convey."

"What about the men still alive? Elder Sa would have handed them over to the imperials. Is that... best?"

"Is your real question whether Sa's strict but straightforward idea trumps Ci's covert plotting?"

"Um... sort of. I mean, there's right and wrong but I... don't know which is which anymore. When this discord was between imperials and E Mo, I thought I knew. Was it really after all, clashing ideologies between the E Mo, refueling the old wars between Demons and Demon Slayers, or a ruse by one of Wang Liang's follower to destabilize Zhang Tang's new government? Maybe it's everything. This triumph over Ci's army doesn't feel a victory. Sa died for her views. While I respect her opinions, as I look back now, I can't say that I wholeheartedly agree."

"I don't think either was right. Neither were they wrong. The E Mo need to relinquish wounds from the past but letting the imperials treat them like dirt isn't doing anyone favors. Both elders were stubborn fools who could have solved this properly had their emotions been placed aside."

"Don't you think Elder Sa was more objective?"

"Was she? I might be inclined to believe that if Cai Yun weren't her granddaughter. I imagine this clash was her method to punish Ming Na for Cai Yun's death. It's doubtful Ci expected the ambush. That Demon-inducing powder was probably a last resort to fend off the invasion."

"That's crazy. H-How are you certain Sa was Cai Yun's grandmother?"

"Through Yang and passing conversations I picked up here and there. People weren't discreet when they thought I couldn't understand their language."

"Oh, no! Yang! I forgot about him! Send help. He's badly injured!"

"The Ji Lin folks have him in their care, along with that vile-tongued woman. They're holding her until Lu's generals come."

"Thank goodness. Wait, Yang knew Elder Sa was Cai Yun's grandmother? No wonder he was on his best behavior!"

"What are you talking about?"

"After you and Li Li ran off, Yang wanted to confront Ci in Ming Na but I wouldn't let him. I took him to Er Na and confided in Elder Sa... which must have substantiated her suspicions against Ci. She came to put down the rebellion which means... this was my fault."

"It's not your fault. I wanted to protect you so I purposefully kept things to myself."

"You, what? Talk about putting emotions aside for objectivity! You could have trusted me!"

"I know. I'm sorry. Thing could have turned out differently if I'd relied on you."

"W-Well... According to Elder Gui, this is how things should end, as Heaven dictates."

"You don't really believe that, do you?"

"After all the insanity I've witnessed, anything is possible."

"Such as?"

"Such as unknowingly giving Hei Se Fa Ling to a latent Demon who would move the world if it meant saving you. By the way, is Li Li still gloating about how much better she is than me?"

"She hasn't even gloated once. Too busy convincing her skeptical brother that she could save anyone."

"Oh. Well, then... never mind. My memories are a bit hazy. I'm pretty sure you saved me so, thank you. You become more amazing each day, Doctor."

"I won't take credit for Bai Hu's merits."

"I can taste willow, Dui. And, I haven't forgotten this strange heaviness on my chest. You saved me using Yu Qi's chi control technique, didn't you?"

Half-shrugging, Dui looks away. The pink hue lacing his cheeks makes him rather adorable from his angle.

Six months ago, he knew next to nothing about chi treatments. All those times he inquired about the techniques Yu Qi used to save me, along with his recent shift from studying modern to traditional methods, I thought he simply meant to surpass his brother. In actuality, he was planning ahead because in his sentiment, peace is the result of battered nations unable to wage war. Should war return, I would be inclined to offer my bloodline advantage for Nan Rong's safety. Dui was looking out for me. He always does. That's why I love him. His convictions, kindness, loyalty, and intelligence are what I love most about him. I may not always agree with his decisions but I will always respect Dui. This distance between us is another of those decisions I will respect.

"Regardless of what you did or didn't do, thank you, Dui."

"Don't mention it," he mutters, turning redder by the second. "You're stable now. I'm going to examine those men. There might be a safe way to cleanse the drug from their systems."

"Be careful."

Chapter 13 – 2

Three days later, survivors from the vicious clash, Pak Teng, along with a group of Ji Lin outcasts, gather in Er Na. Out of Sa's army, ten survived. Ming Na lost over half their people. More could have scattered during the raid but aren't likely to return after this tragedy. A handful of warriors from Yue Na who joined Ci's ranks also perished, leaving all three cities to mourn. Ironically, the most miserable person amongst them can't shed a tear. He's gone mute. Despite having survived, his soul is nowhere near. The path of blood chosen to save the E Mo nearly destroyed them, which ultimately, destroyed him. For now, Elder Ci waits for judgment in Er Na's dungeon.

With Dui's treatment, many who took the berserker powder lived to repent for their crimes. Cowards who couldn't stand the consequences of their actions left the E Mo, those strong stayed behind to provide support for the wounded with every expectation of receiving punishment. Whatever that punishment will be is unclear. Dui is of neutral opinion, in that he doesn't wish to interfere. After some deliberation, Hu and I both concede to that opinion.

"U-U-Uh... um. Miss. That man woke up." He tugs at my sleeve in an adorable, shy manner, befitting the young boy that he is. The streak of rouge across round cheeks and averted eyes make him even more endearing. I don't blame him for feeling awkward; after all, he tried to kill me.

"Hmm? Which one?"

"The ugly one."

"Which ugly one?"

"Y-You know, the one you said to call for you when he wakes!"

Caught off guard, the child called Fu Ping looks up. Spotting my grin, Fu Ping quickly glances down again. I ruffle his hair, to which he frowns, while relaxing tense shoulders. With his sister's killer in custody, a sense of contentment washed over the poor boy. He wants to apologize, but can't find the courage, and so Fu Ping has been dawdling near me all day asking for tasks one after the other.

"Thanks Fu-Fu. You've been a big help. This makes us even now, okay?"

"It's *Fu Ping*!"

"Okay! Geez! We're basically finished here. Why don't you go outside and play?"

"I'm not a kid and I'm not leaving! What else do you need?"

"No? Sure look like a brat to me. Listen, kid. I don't have time to babysit you. It's exhausting. Go help Master Dui. He needs more bandages... Fu-Fu."

"You—! You're a real dummy!"

Well, that did it. He's stormed off. It's getting late and Fu Ping's clearly tired. Hopefully, he'll listen to Dui and rest.

"Certainly have a way with children, don't you, *Dummy*?"

"Shut your mouth, Yang."

Turning around, I make my way over to the ugly patient Fu Ping was guarding, who has fully emerged from stupor. The once handsome face is battered and bruised. Lacerations cover his body. He'd lost so much blood, I thought he didn't stand a chance. Somehow, Dui was able to stabilize his vitals. For the past three days, Yang's been in and out of consciousness, mostly mumbling nonsense and calling for Cai Yun.

"Is she dead?"

"What a grim question. No. Zhang Rai is in Lu's custody."

"Good. Death would be too kind."

"Calm down. Your heart rate's elevating."

"I'm not afraid to die."

"Oh, good. Then I won't feel bad if you do. Listen, loudmouth, survivors from Sa's army praised your valiance. Whether you like it or not, you're the new 'Champion of the Savages.'"

"No thanks."

"Like I said, you don't have a choice. So, what happened, Yang? Why did Sa lead her men to Ming Na?"

"Are you pointing fingers?"

"Not at all. I know Ci's Demons flanked Sa's party. You tried to save her and singlehandedly dispatched the ambush. Playing the hero didn't come without cost. The survivors said they left you behind because they thought you wouldn't make it. What I don't understand is why her party advanced on Ming Na in the first place. I thought she would have been busy interrogating the missing women's lovers. Also, how did you know where I was?"

"Why should I tell you anything?"

"Because the draught Dui gave you to dull the pain will wear off soon. If you want another, I'll have my answers."

"Sadistic witch."

"Sadistic apothecary. Go on. What happened?"

Snarling, Yang averts attention toward the wall. For a time, we remain silent with Yang sighing heavily while I change his bandages. Eventually, as forewarned, effects from Dui's draught wears off and then the loudmouth continues griping. After nearly an hour spent wincing, Yang grudgingly concedes.

So it goes that when Elder Sa called on the missing women's lovers, they had already defected to Ci's ranks. She went to take them back from Ming Na and became the first casualty of the ambush. As for Yang, truth is stranger than fiction. He swears an old man, whose description eerily resembled Elder Gui, lifted him from the ground and led him to Mue Ran. Yang could have lied. Instincts tell me to trust him.

At the end of our conversation, Dui's draught fully made an impression. When asked if he would return to Bei Ling once his wounds heal, Yang shook his head.

"I'm going to stick around for a while and learn their secret pepper sauce recipe," he said. After that, he began humming aloud and that's when I made a hasty retreat.

Chapter 14: Bravery from the Heart

"Hey, you."

The day's gone by quickly. I finished making the usual rounds in the infirmary and decided to pay the cultivation area a visit. Dui was busy teaching new apprentices. I didn't want to interrupt. He's gain numerous admirers, most of whom crowd the doctor as had the women back in Pa Xu. Dui's become as popular as another Southern celebrity who's approaching forthwith.

"Hey, to you too, Bai Hu. That outfit suits you."

Blushing, the Demon General looks away and hurriedly scratches his head. Since his clothes were soaked in blood, Er Na's fawning ladies offered to wash them and he's left wearing traditional E Mo warrior garb, which I heard the same ladies also insisted. The fur is a nice touch. His partially exposed muscular chest is enough to make any lady swoon. He certainly is the spitting image of valiant Chief Cao Sung.

"Are you all better?"

"Yeah, I'm fine. Thanks. What about you?"

"The Demon General won't be bested by a bunch of fakes."

"I mean it, Hu. Your injuries were severe. I was really scared. What happened back there? Have you lost the Demon's power?"

Frowning, he shuffles and sways as if not knowing what to say. Hu dislikes feeling weak and powerless. His inability to diverge from the masculine image might have partially been stemmed from our childhood, when I teased him about his height and weak arms. He also feels guilty for having been unable to fully protect me. Until I've reassured him that my prodding is purely out of concern and not reprisal, Hu circles the answer.

Sighing, Hu scratches his head for the fifth time. "I've been unstable since you left."

"Unstable?"

"Sometimes, I'm more powerful than ever and other times, I can't use my advantage at all. It's been a confusing six months. I started feeling like my old self again shortly after you left and that's when this happened. Master Zhuang thinks that I'm subconsciously working through some things, whatever that means."

"I'm sorry. I hope you'll be all right."

"I'm fine. Just takes time."

"Right. Promise me you'll be careful."

"I will. I really will be fine, Bao Lai." He nods emphatically.

"Thank you. How did things go at the summit?"

"Besides from trying not to draw attention to my embarrassing costume? It went well. Ci and Zhang Rai were hauled off to the capital for trial and the three kidnapped victims were returned to their families. They're due in Sai Mi in a few weeks to give their account, but it seems that Rai told Governor Lu everything."

"She did?"

"Hmm. She said there was nothing wrong with telling the truth once in a while. I guess she abducted those women so their enraged lovers would join Ci. When some were 'too stubborn,' she had their women killed."

"Weren't there more fake Demons than the number of women kidnapped?"

"Fear brought a large number of volunteers into Ci's services. The thing is, she never told Ci about the kidnappings; so, she said. The whole farce was her idea, meant to destroy the imperials and the E Mo. The latter were despised by Wang Liang. The former turned their backs on his authority. That is one crazy loyal woman."

"Do you think Ci was really ignorant? Will Zhang Tang show him leniency?"

"Who knows?" Hu shrugs. "Zhang Tang is fair-minded. Let him decide."

"Right. So, what's next for Ming Na and Er Na?"

"For now, survivors are to stay here in Er Na. The Minister of Foreign Affairs will be arriving soon from Sai Mi. She'll decide how to proceed with Ming Na's reconstructions after meeting with the elders. Oh, you'll like this. Li Li is Ming Na's new chief elder. The decision was unanimous."

"R-Really?! Wow! That is interesting. She must be the youngest one ever!"

"Saving everyone has its perks."

"Seriously! Mo Bi must be proud and terribly jealous. What about Er Na? Who's going to replace Elder Sa?"

"Me, if the council has their way. Cao Sung this and Cao Sung that. I know we look alike and all but... I'm not interested in wearing *this* for the rest of my life."

"Ha! You do look good in it though. Hey, Hu, I've been meaning to ask. Do you know if you're E Mo?"

Shrugging, a pensive glance flies north toward the tall statue of the broad-shouldered man. Hu was an orphan, his lineage is a mystery. When we met at Tian Mao Yi, he only knew his own name, and he wasn't sure who gave it to him.

"Hu—"

That's odd. I hadn't realized it until now. The very object that's been right before my eyes, the twin tiger bell pendant around his neck, the one that has always been there as long as I can remember, is the same one carved onto Chief Cao Sung's statue. Hu's name also means tiger. Aside from their uncanny resemblance, Hu's strength proves blood ties to the Demon tribes. On top of everything, the caravan was able to reach Ming Na quickly without going through Mue Ran because Hu's instinct brought them to a lost trail. He seems to know his way around too well. It's possible that he's not related to the great warrior Cao Sung. There's a greater possibility that he is. I know he's realized that too.

"Are you going to stay for a while?"

"Hmm?" He turns back, eyes still glazed from wonder. "N-Nah. I have duties in Nan Rong. Sitting on a throne all day is not my idea of fun. The E Mo needs to stop idolizing some dead guy and move on."

"That's... one way to put it."

"What about you? What are you going to do?"

"Go home, I guess."

"Which home? My offer's still on the table. My home will always be your home. I've not always been myself but I have always loved you, Bao Lai. Not one day goes by that I don't think about you. I shouldn't have waited this long to make things official. Come back to An. I want to make you my wife."

"Hu... you're very sweet and I do love you, I always will, but..."

"You love him more."

"It's not a matter of love. I love you both. You both mean the world to me. I can't thank you enough for loving me, Hu. It was you who showed me what love is and what it means to love. I'll treasure every precious memory from our path in life together. My choice was made six months ago. From here and for the rest of my life, the path ahead for me is with Dui. You keep me safe. He makes me brave. He makes me look forward even when it's easier to turn back. I want to be there for him. That is something I couldn't do for you. I hope you'll find a love more deserving."

For someone not typically emotional, Hu's eyes are red. I feel like crying but can't; otherwise, he'll take my tears as doubt and cling onto false hope. I've gone a long way to make the same choice. This time, I don't feel any notion of regret.

"Tsk." Sighing sharply, wavering eyes look to the west where the red sun is slowly setting, giving off golden and crimson hues. His shoulders tremble ever so slightly. For a long while, we bask in the sun's glow together just as we had those many years ago at Tian Mao Yi. Same as then, this moment together will forever be etched into my memory.

Just as the last of the sun recedes below the horizon, he turns back and lets out a long sigh. "The one time you decide to sound romantic is when you're saying good-bye. I'll respect your choice but what are you planning to do? He's still ignoring you."

"That's okay. He'll come around and we'll return to the way we were."

"Master and apprentice?"

"For now. When we left An, Dui and I made a pact to marry in twenty years should we remain single. It's been nearly one. For Dui, I can wait nineteen more."

"Hmph. He brings out the romantic in you, doesn't he?"

"Maybe."

"Something I couldn't do."

"Well, you were romantic enough for the both of us. Sweet, protective, and passionate too. Someday soon, a very lucky woman will have your attention, Bai Hu. I hope she'll make you very happy. I wish nothing more than for your happiness."

"Speak for yourself. Wherever you go, whatever you want to do, be happy, Bao Lai."

"I will."

Wonderful big arms envelop all of me in a loving embrace. Everything that is Bai Hu is indescribably nostalgic. We've known each other for so long, have loved each other for so long, that accepting this may be the last time we are this way rips at my heart. Still, I'm glad we could have this chance meeting to properly say good-bye. I needed to know that he'll be all right.

Throughout the long embrace, exchanging warmth gives no consequence to time. Once we slowly part, stars have come out in droves. The cold air has no effects between our affections, same as distance between our hearts. No matter which paths we take, Xiao Meow and Little Hung, Bai Hu and Bao Lai, will always have this unbreakable bond.

Hu's melancholy smile is also encouraging. I feel the same smile spread across my own mouth. The time has finally come. This is where we part.

"I guess this is it then. I'm going to get my clothes back from those evasive ladies and prepare for departure. Can't believe how time flies. It's spring again. It'll be interesting to see the types of recruits Qing Hai brings in. He had better not picked any boastful wimps."

"Don't be too hard on Qing Hai. He's doing his best."

"Did he complain to you? Tsk! I'll triple his duties in the barracks!"

"He's not your trainee anymore, Bai Hu."

"That's what he thinks!"

"Ha-ha! I'll have to apologize to Qing Hai now that he's earned your wrath. I'm sure he did well. Turn those new recruits into respectable warriors, General. Well, I know you will. I'm proud to call Nan Rong home because of honorable soldiers like you. I'm proud of *you*, Bai Hu."

"Don't make me blush."

"Ha! Right. Have a safe trip back."

"You too."

After squeezing my hand a few times, Hu starts for the city center. I watch him go, sad and also relieved. A quarter of the way down the road, he pauses. "Oh, one more thing. Dui had better not make you cry or I'll make him regret it. You hear me, Dui? Don't think I'll forgive you just because she does."

"Dui—?"

Before I can finish, Hu marches off, leaving me in dismay as I whip about, lips half parted and shoulders tensed. From behind one of the tall walls, which encircle the cultivated pots filled with fruiting plants, Dui slowly emerges with hands in his pockets. The complicated expression shields his opinions. Evasive eyes glance over and just as quickly, look away again.

For a drawn moment, silence saturates the air. I fumble about for something to say while he seems to be doing his best to avoid conversations altogether.

"A-Are you... h-have you... um—did you need—um, what I mean is—did... you... ugh. I don't know anymore!"

Smacking his lips quietly, the doctor withdraws hands from the shirt pockets and then leisurely folds them across his chest. Dui looks over, brimming with an emotion I can't describe.

"This is your plan? Wait nineteen more years and then coerce me through a joke made in passing?"

"M-Maybe. Unless you happen to marry someone else."

"You would let me marry someone else?"

"Probably not. No. Definitely not. Not without throwing the greatest tantrum you'll ever witness. I might even steal the groom away on his wedding night."

"Heh. Then if the groom doesn't have a choice but to marry this possessive woman, he'd rather not wait another day."

"Erm... what?"

"Is that your answer?"

"Wh—? No! I mean yes! Wait, what?"

"The E Mo have an old tradition. Under the light of the new moon, should a woman accept a man's hand and then together walk around the fire thrice, their past, present, and future are bound. Tonight is the new moon. I'll wait for you by the bonfire. Give me your answer then."

"W-Wait! D-Don't walk away so suddenly! Dui!"

Above, the pale moon is starting to show her ivory face. That was a proposal, I think, and he's giving me no time at all to prepare. My answer is obvious and yet, somehow, I feel a little cheated. This was more than a mere jump; more so, a leap across a canyon. How can he go from rejecting me to inference of a proposal, one that's slated in a few hours?

"Ugh, I can't wear this."

The pink robe, the symbol of Hu's affection for me which I've worn fondly, not only would feel inappropriate for the occasion, but is also faded, tattered and covered in blood stains. My face is dirty and my hair is messy from running about in the infirmary. I didn't even pack a comb.

"I can help, Miss Bao Lai."

"You too?! How long have you been standing there, Li Li?"

"Long enough," she giggles. Li Li moves from behind another wall opposing Dui's former hiding place. Ming Na's new chief elder is sporting some rather exotic fur. She appears more of an adult, carrying Elder Gui's outlook and Elder Sa's temperament, along with Chief Cao Sung's immeasurable strength. Given her age and talent, Li Li has all the time needed to return peace to the E Mo.

"Um... Congratulations. I just heard the news. And also, thanks for saving my behind. Oh, here, I best give this to you before I forget. Elder Gui said this piece together with yours are called Ping Jing Fa Ling. We don't need these in the wrong hands again."

"Thanks. I'll keep them both safe. And, you're welcome, though honestly, I was only trying to save Master Dui."

"Well, I figured that much. I hope you're not brokenhearted over Dui."

Frowning, the young chief elder rolls those big jade eyes. "You're slow, aren't you, Miss Bao Lai?"

"What is that supposed to mean?"

"I was never in love with Master Dui. I'm grateful he saved me of course. My affection for him is purely derived from respect."

"Is that right?"

"Come now, Miss Bao Lai. If I were serious about Master Dui, you wouldn't stand a chance. After all, I am better than you in every way. Younger, prettier, smarter, and stronger too."

She's joking, I hope. Not that she would be wrong to make such bold claims but that's a level of conceit not suited for a young girl.

"Uh-huh. You've already fondled him publicly to no avail. How much farther would you have gone?"

"It was for his sake. He looked so sad when he came in. I asked him why. He wouldn't say much. Then I figured things out so I took it upon myself to make you jealous."

"Er... You do know *he* rejected *me*, right?"

"Just because Master Dui is a man doesn't mean that he should give in so easily. You have to earn his love. If you can't see that, I'm not so sure you're good enough for him yet."

"Who are you, his mother?"

"Elder Gui said fate brought him to Ming Na. To this day Master Dui doesn't remember how he first stumbled into our city. His mother died shortly before I was born. He couldn't save her. In turn, he saved me when no one else could. So, you see, anything's possible."

"That's disturbing. I'm going to... back away slowly now."

"Very funny, Miss Bao Lai. We have a wedding to plan. Come along."

"Hey, wait! When the heck did you get so strong? Stop tugging, you'll rip my arm off!"

Chapter 14 – 2

The wedding gown is vibrant and lovely, so are the headdress, embroidered shoes, and makeup painted on my face. Li Li and a handful of ladies from Ji Lin prepared every detail. I must appear a tribal princess and it's absolutely embarrassing. Not once since we've been together have I looked so dolled up. In fact, I might have purposefully been more of slob around Dui. He's not superficial. I never worried over presentation. If only I had, my face wouldn't be scorched red in this moment.

At the opposite end of the courtyard, Dui is smiling brightly in the bridegroom ensemble. His hair is clipped back to fully show the handsome features. The defined nose, rosy lips, and wonderfully beautiful grey eyes make him rival any dashing prince. Just one glance and my heart is in my throat. The sight absolutely takes my breath away.

"Ahem!" Giggling, Li Li pushes me forward at the same time Mo Bi pushes Dui.

It seems after realizing my frailty, Mo Bi has gotten over his boyish adulation, and instead come to devote his time to caring for a most important sister. Ming Na's new chief elder aims to unite the outcasts on Ji Lin Hills and the E Mo, starting with a celebration under the new moon. Pak Teng's cheerful barking from afar is calling for festivities to begin.

Smiling, the pair leaves the courtyard for the bonfire near Chief Cao Sung's statue. I watch them go, thankful to have met such good friends, thankful for all the tears and laughter that lead us to this moment. Despite everything that's happened, the future for the E Mo is not isolation. It is bright and full of hope. For Dui and for me, our part in this story is complete. A new chapter waits in Nan Rong. A new life together. However, there is still another matter to settle before the curtains to this act are drawn.

"You look beau—Ouch! What was that for?"

"You have some nerve, Dui! Where do you get off proposing to me out of the blue?"

"I'm... sorry?"

Still rubbing his arm where my fist landed, Dui looks down wide-eyed and confused. I don't know why I did that. My body won't stop trembling. I feel like crying and smiling at once. I love him, that is indisputable, and it makes me mad!

"You're sorry because it was a mistake."

"Of course not! I have never been more serious!"

"Why? Why now? You've been avoiding me for months before I ever confessed and then when I poured out my heart, you rejected me. Earlier this morning, you wouldn't even look at me! What's changed in the last twelve hours? What is this really about? Are you really afraid I'll coerce marriage from you in nineteen years? It was a joke! Don't make yourself miserable to spare my feelings!"

"I'm not—!"

"No? *Oh, now I understand!* You thought I'd choose Bai Hu. Since I didn't, you're self-sacrificing so I don't become a spinster, right? I haven't forgotten your lectures. 'Get marry. Start a family. Stop throwing your life away. You're not getting any younger!' Well, I don't need your pity, Dui!"

"I don't—I love you!"

"Great! You just don't want to be with me, that's all! *Fine!* Pretend I never said anything!"

"Just—hold on a minute! Where are you going?"

"Home! And don't follow me either! I need time to get over you... get used to pretending I'm over you. I'll come back to Pa Xu and finish my apprenticeship when I'm damn well ready!"

"Your home *is* in Pa Xu."

"My house is near Kou. What are you doing? Let go, Dui. Don't make me kick you!"

"Your home is with me, Bao Lai!"

I can't breathe. I can't see anything aside from dark fluttering lashes brushing against my own. His suffocating kiss to silence all protest is robbing every bit of air from my lungs. The arms constricting my waist grow more fervent by the second. I can't breathe but I also can't find the will to withdraw. My head is swimming from the ardent passion. Every moment goes by makes me crave more of him. Busy hands of the once lecherous doctor fall back to their old ways, crawling up the entire length of my back to my shoulders and face, before moving down and cupping lower cheeks. Six months ago, I would have threatened to break his hands, and now I... can't recall why I was yelling six seconds ago.

Each fervent moment brings unbridled chills, making the retreat that much more painful, though I don't know how much longer we could have endured. Our foreheads bump together wearily upon withdrawal while we both gasp desperately for air. The taste of his lips lingers a sweet sensation, same as the warmth from the embrace.

A tender whisper escapes rose red lips; my name, a pleasing echo from his mouth. High spirits. Intoxicated delirium. I feel as though I'll fall off the face of the earth if he ever lets go.

Lowered grey eyes of a somnambulist capture all of me, entirely. He smiles, leans down to kiss my forehead, and then through half-parted lips, search for fleeting thoughts to express the indescribable sensation filling our souls. In his place, I've only one declaration to offer.

"I love you."

Simple words, that's all they are. Words he's heard before and yet, still awestruck as if hearing the confession for the first time. The gentle, affectionate smile is one I've missed dearly; the smile of a man who worships me as I've come to worship him. This is my Dui at last.

"You have very poor taste in men."

"Are you rejecting me?"

"I might have lost my mind from jealousy but rejecting the single person I have ever loved this way would be pure insanity." Sighing softly, a grin quickly fades from the cheerful face. "Sorry. I saw Bai Hu kissed you after the first summit and I let myself succumbed to envy. I didn't mean any of the cruel words that came after."

"You were spying then too? Bai Hu caught me off guard. What was I supposed to do, pummel him senseless?"

"That might not have been a bad idea."

"You say that, Dui, but I don't think you were ever jealous. Jealous men rush to win their beloveds, not push them toward another. I hope this hasn't been another compulsive attempt at humoring me. Think things over. You've been increasingly unhappy. Most days when we sit together, your attention is out the window. Before today, you hadn't smiled for months. Is this really how you want to spend the rest of your life?"

Exhaling quietly, his gaze falls in the usual avoiding manner. The sad expression is back. I knew it. He always defaults to indulging my fancy.

"It's okay, Dui. Don't push yourself. I understand that my admission came unexpected. If I'd shown you one fraction of intimacy beforehand, demanding your eternal devotion wouldn't have been as insulting. Fact is, I thought about approaching you a million times, and then each time, I pushed the chance aside because I thought there would be another. I assumed too much. Affections change—"

"Yes, they do. For nearly the past year, my world has revolved around one belligerent woman who's grown accustomed to tormenting me. My boyish obsession has become something unbearable. I never thought I would love anyone, let alone fall this deeply for a person I thought I could never have. The more I loved you, the more distraught and empty life became. I wanted to run but I couldn't accept being away from you. So, I resigned myself to burying these affections the only way I knew how. If I was mute, it was to keep from screaming my frustration. If I was distant, it was to keep from crying."

The hard gaze burrowing into the ground grows tremulous. Dui's on the verge of tears. I've never seen him cry but I know I've heard his tears. These arms around my body; the strained voice. While I lied dying in Ming Na, the one who called me back from the abyss was Dui. He cried for me, suffered for me, and without hesitation, threw himself over me as a mean to deflect Ci's assault. Dui's always willing to forfeit life and limb for my sake.

It's not how severe a man desires that shows his love and devotion, it's how severe he suffers. Any fool can love. Only a true lover grieves. These were Zhang Rai's cynicism. Although I can't fully agree with her harsh view, there is something morbidly noble about suffering for the sake of love.

We've been together for some time now while secretly, Dui was truly alone. I was contented to have a friend and in turn, undermined his loneliness. Dui might have kept his affections silent, but each time he pushed me toward the idea of marriage was merely another confession, same as when I teased him about his multitude of admirers.

Having been blind to his suffering for so long, it was insensitive to assert my feelings and forced him to undo the wall placed around his heart in one fell swoop. Up until today, my heart was split in two. Dui couldn't give me all of him until I was willing to give him all of me. At this moment, we belong to each other.

Dui looks up when two hands cup his cheeks. Sadness in grey eyes slowly dissipates when my arms wrap around his neck to convey every thought left unheard through a lingering kiss. The warmth of his body gives rise to the familiar scent I'll always recognize as home. My home is wherever he is, for the next nineteen years and every second thereafter.

"Pfff, haha! What a dirty look you have on your face, Dui!"

"Bai Hu was right. You're not very romantic."

Frowning, his lips fully withdraw. The strong arms are still wrapped around my waist, proof that he will not relinquish me any time soon. For that, I'm grateful.

"So, how about it, love? Will you accept my hand and stroll three times around the bonfire?"

'Love' and 'dove' were Dui's usual terms of endearment for every woman, back when he couldn't keep travelling hands to himself. Perversion has gone from his tone but those hands have resumed their travels. One is cupping my lower cheek now.

"I don't think so, Doctor. I'd rather have the ceremony at Tian Mao Yi so that Master Tai Hung can attend. I think he'll appreciate seeing his two pups join hands."

"For a thought that fastidious, you must have planned this for a while, love."

"Nuh-uh! W-W-What are you talking about? I-I never planned our wedding inside my head."

"No? I have."

"Seriously?"

"Yup. Down to the tablecloth. Grey's a good color."

"No way! I want blue! I-I mean... "

Darn it! He caught me and he's gloating through that triumphant grin. I'm happy to see his smile again and ecstatic to know this is one of millions to come.

"Blue tablecloths. I'll keep that in mind. And here, you dropped this. That is, I dropped it, you found it and then you dropped it, and I found it. We're equally clumsy."

"My Dui panda! I almost forgot him!"

"You named the panda, Dui?"

"Yes, because he looks just like you. Disinterested and adorable."

"Thanks, I think. I'll sew him on another blanket once we're home."

"Thanks, Dui. You're the best."

"Of course, I am. Took you long enough to realize it."

Grinning, we walk hand in hand toward the gathering near Chief Cao Sung's statue. There won't be a wedding this night. However, this night is still reserved for unions. The E Mo have come together as one. The outcasts on Ji Lin have made new friends. And me, I've found that which I've been missing: a place by the side of this wonderful person who gives my life purpose.

Above, stars twinkle jovially in the diamond-laced sky, each carrying a message I'll never know. Fate is a curious thing. Maybe, life without mystery would lead to stagnation. Elder Gui never had a chance to tell me who was most distraught over my retreat from the yurt that first day. Now, I know whom I'd be most distraught without. Where we go from here is the destiny of our choices.

"One more thing. Why did Li Li come to me earlier and said Yu Ling only forced the unreasonable promise out of motherly concern? As long as I'm happy, she couldn't care less if I don't marry by thirty."

"Erm... I never told Li Li about your promise to your mother and I definitely didn't tell her your mother's name."

"How did she...?"

"There's a running theory but you won't believe it."

Chapter 15: A Night to Remember

Gosh, it's good to be home! I've missed the noxious scent of dried herbs and tonics. Nan Rong's climate is perfect and the weather today is exceeding comfortable, sunny and cool. I never want to see another desert so long as I live.

"Where are Gai and Wan? The clinic shouldn't have closed for another few hours."

"They're practicing over at Hua's until we reopen. I had Bai Hu send my letter when he left. Figured we'd need a day or two to recover from the exhausting trip."

"Suddenly you two are friends. Notice how you don't scowl anymore each time his name comes out of your mouth?"

"Bai Hu is an honorable man. Respecting a rival is not unheard of."

"Especially, since you've won, huh?"

"That too."

Dui drops the heavy satchel onto the hardwood floor. Soon after landing in a thud, my back echoes a similar sound from being pushed against the door. The doctor's ravenous lips seek to devour mine. Indiscretion sends his travelling hands over every inch of me within reach. I can't fathom the extent of his desire and yet, once I begin to let myself drown beneath the passion, Dui moves back, flushed and fidgety.

"What's wrong, Doctor?"

"Nothing. I... I—*ahem*—I forgot something at the trade shop. W-Why don't you rest while I... anyway, don't wait up."

And he's out the door.

Chapter 15 – 2

A sinewy hand silences the little bell on the door. The bauble pauses and then as though fretting, jingles gently once or twice. It's a little past midnight. He's been absent since late afternoon. Cold night air has turned the complexion blushed pink. The shadow glances across the floor to the low table where dinner is cold before carefully tiptoeing into the backroom.

"Dui!"

"Hmm?!" He flips around, fumbling the satchel in hand, though miraculously makes a last minute save.

"Why are you still up?"

"What's in the bag, Dui?"

"Here I thought you lost sleep because of me. Should I feel jealous?"

"Is it empty again?"

"Of course not."

"May I see it?"

"No. What is this about?"

"That's what I'd like to know. I'm trying not to take offense but it's difficult when you keep running off every time we kiss. Er Na was the exception. I'm guessing because we nearly died and you were jealous of Bai Hu. Now that we're free from the emotional whirlwind, if you've changed your mind, I'll understand. Don't run. Talk to me. I'm not going anywhere."

"My intentions haven't changed. I love you."

"I'm not questioning your love. Your lust, or lack thereof, worries me. What I mean is... have you thought this through?"

"You'll have to be more precise than that."

"What I'm trying to say is... imply is... are we... compatible?"

"Again, you'll have to be more precise than that."

"Darn it! This is... Don't hate me for bringing this up! Remember when you confided in me on Mount Chou about your first relationship and how things couldn't *advance* in that manner because of your peculiarity with women? The thought's been nudging at my psyche. I'm scared of losing you over something as trivial as intimacy. You don't have to run away. I've decided that come what may, I'm happy as long as we're together. If mere companionship wasn't your expectation, we'll find another way. I'll do whatever it takes!"

"Are you quite finished?"

"Hmm?"

"What kind of person do you take me for? I would never propose on a whim. My first relationship should have ended before it began. I didn't love her. Felt

286

absolutely nothing for her. The more I forced what wasn't there, the more miserable I became. Maybe the entire ordeal was subconsciously executed; an excuse to end a failing attachment. On the other hand, I was miserable over you from denial. Each time you come into view, I have the urge to examine every inch of your body for medically unnecessary reasons, I'm ashamed to say. Here. This was supposed to be a surprise but since my manhood is in question, I don't have a choice."

From the satchel, he draws a luxurious red embroidered silk box into my hand. "Open it."

"I don't know if I want to when you're this miffed."

"You've already insulted me, what's the harm? Go on."

Dui's half smirk almost resembles a grimace. At this point, even should I refuse, he'll open the box anyway. Curiosity is getting the better of me. There's really no point to resist.

"Oh my... Dui... they're beautiful. Beautiful and *expensive!* Are you nuts? How much did these cost?!"

"My wife deserves the very best that I can provide. Our engagement is once in a lifetime. I don't plan to marry anyone else, ever. I will never love anyone but you."

Inside the dimly lit room, the gold drop earrings inlaid with rubies sparkle as brightly as stars in dark skies. Around the edges are intricate patterns, clearly refined with care by a talented artisan. At the base, large dangling rubies resemble petals of a rose. A pair fit for nobility. Above the surreal beauty of the earrings, rubies represent powerful, unending love. They're a popular gemstone for engagements and weddings, the reality of which finally dawn on me.

"I love you, too. Tsk! You're going to make me cry, Dui! That's really sweet! Thank you so much for thinking of me but are you sure we can afford these?"

"Minister San An was very generous with my severance pay. We have plenty left for rainy days. Besides, they were specially ordered. I can't return them. Not that I would even bother after having to endure two hours of interrogation by that spiteful buffoon while his men supposedly unloaded the shipment. He finally retrieved the box from under the counter when I threatened to take my money back."

"Two hours? Where were you the rest of the day?"

"Finding blue tablecloths, amongst other things. I talked to the head priest at Tian Mao Yi. He's agreed to marry us in three days."

"Three days?! That's not enough time to prepare! We have to make invitations, t-the wedding gowns, food, decorations—"

"All taken care of. Make that, all except for a place to spend our wedding night. I was thinking a pavilion by

Lake Xiang or somewhere in the mountains. What do you think?"

"I think I... can't wait to be your wife."

Never in my life could I imagine being engaged to a man so sweet. I don't know what I did to deserve him. I'm just happy that he's mine. Words can't begin to describe this elation welling inside and so, without words, my arms fling around his neck to bring us closer. Deepening kisses. Bodies pressed together tightly. I can feel his heart beat through the many layers while racing pulse pour forth heat that seeks to burn an imprint onto my skin. Even then, the single thought racing through my mind is that we're not close enough. The moment I reach to undo his shirt, the doctor jumps back, scratching his head furiously.

"Boy, it sure is late! We've both had a tiring day. Let's turn in for the night. I'll see you in the morning! Goodnight, Bao Lai!"

"You have got to be kidding me! Are you running away again?!"

"It's past midnight."

"And? The clinic's not open tomorrow."

"I'm... tired?"

"Oh. Your urge to examine every inch of my body for medically unnecessary reasons is thwarted by fatigue. Makes sense. Too bad I'm not in the least bit tired and I've suddenly the urge to examine every inch of your body for medically unnecessary reasons."

"H-Hey, wait! Stop, Bao Lai! Your enthusiasm is much appreciated but give a little consideration to my poor heart. I won't be able to stop myself—"

"Who said you had to stop?"

"Excuse me? You were serious? *My god, woman!* Have a little decency! We're not married yet!"

"Pfff, ha ha! That's so cute! I had no idea the doctor with travelling hands was old-fashioned. Then again, I should have known. You were also prim and proper when we were children. Glad some things haven't changed. But um, since you've never... and then there *was* your peculiarity with women... don't you want to know if we're actually compatible?"

"I'm this close to losing my mind from your ill-mannered groping. I really don't need the experiment."

"Prude. Does it matter when we're engaged? Three days early won't make a difference."

"Stop trying to corrupt me. I was taught to be a gentleman. You won't have my chastity this night, vixen."

For Dui, I would have waited another nineteen years. At this point, teasing him is enough to satisfy my bad habit of tormenting him; though, I haven't finished just yet. A sultry smile. A sensual stroke up the length of his arm. My hands traverse from the reddened cheeks on his face to those below his waist. Puckered lips beg for a sweet kiss. The rises of my chest press against his shivering body.

"Have I told you, Doctor Dui, that my fantasies have recently run wild from all sorts of dirty deeds, all of which include you in some very naughty arrangements? I can't sleep, can't eat, and whenever I see you, I'm overcome by fever. Have you anything to treat my suffering? I would do anything to relinquish this ache in my heart."

"V-Very funny."

Dui's on the verge of tears. His entire body is trembling from a strained heart. A corner of the rose-colored mouth quivers in a rising arch. Seeing him this way makes the teasing backfire. I'm starting to feel nervous. To top things off, my nerves weren't prepared for this excitement.

"Get back here, Dui!"

"That'll have to suffice for three more days, love!"

The cad tricked me into letting down my guard with a kiss to the cheek. So much for being a gentleman! He darts off after taking no responsibility for stopping my heart from squeezing the protrusions on my chest. I won't let him escape. There's nowhere to run.

"Ack! I'm a doctor, don't hit me!"

"Hitting you isn't punishment enough!"

Past the reception area, into the brewing room, and extra storage closet. Dui slips out the door and makes for the room adjacent. The tall, lanky doctor hasn't lost a step since those days in Nan Rong's services. He's always been agile, so that regardless of space, Dui's able to evade each time I reach out.

"You'll have to do better than that, love."

"Stop moving so fast!"

"Stand still and let a shameless woman take advantage of me? Out of the question! I'm not that easy!"

"Darn it, Dui! Don't make me use Tian Ji Zhong Shi Yan! *Bah!*"

Ouch. I didn't think he'd stop running from the obvious bluff. The next thing I know, we're both on the ground, wincing from the collision.

"Sorry. Are you all right?"

"No... my spleen." He exhales a strained breath. "Why did you have to bring that box along?"

"What box? Oh! I-I'm sorry!"

My engagement present, which I tucked in the breast pocket, slammed into his left side during the fall. Rubbing the point of contact isn't enough. It took some doing to finally dull the pain.

"Dui, are you okay now?"

"Not until you promise me that you won't ever use Tian Ji Zhong Shi Yan unless your life depends on it."

"I wouldn't have used it."

"Don't even joke that way. I don't want to lose you."

My competitive nature shouldn't be underestimated. However, I also won't ever do anything that risks parting from Dui. Never again. This promise is to us both.

Nodding quietly, my face buries into his palm, which rests tremulously upon my cheek. The warmth, scent, and gentle touch are unmistakably Dui. This is the man to whom I've promised my present and future. Our union can't come soon enough.

"Wait a minute. Did you say Guan made you wait two hours before handing over the earrings?"

"The box was under the counter the entire time."

"But, you waited because you thought the shipment just came in, meaning you must have ordered these before leaving for Ming Na."

"That's right."

"Why did you order engagement jewelry when you didn't want a romantic relationship between us?"

"Well..." The good doctor stares off into space, as blushed as a blooming rose. "I did say one of us would come to sense. I knew it would be me. Pettiness can't outlast love. I was lost in indignation, projecting my poor self-view as your opinion. I wanted to believe you'd choose me over Bai Hu, but I was afraid of another rejection. I'm sorry. It was a cowardly attempt to protect my heart."

"For good reasons. To tell the truth, it was inconceivable to think that given another chance, I'd leave Bai Hu. You were right to doubt me because it made me doubt myself until I admitted the unresolved conflict in my heart. Hu and I were once everything to each other, but those days are in the past. They're fond memories and nothing more. You're my everything, Dui. That is true from now until forever."

I can't think else to say and neither can Dui. Words won't change our mutual affections. For a time, comfortable silence imparts a moment of longing gazes. I love him, love everything about him, including Dui's proper disposition.

"You were right. It is getting late. We should turn in."

"No need, love. We're already in your room."

As I push off the floor, Dui plants a passionate kiss and wraps protective arms around my body while exchanging our positions. That's surprising. We are in my room.

"Mmh, Dui, you don't... have to..."

"You caught me. Fair is fair."

"Coercion isn't fair. I admire your virtues and respect your convictions."

"Virtues and convictions are prettier names for stubbornness. Stubbornness nearly led to losing you. I've waited all my life to find this happiness. What's the point in waiting another second? Coerce me, I implore you."

Behind the torrent of love pouring from his eyes is a glimmer of lust growing brighter each passing moment. I've wanted more from Dui. When the moment is near, nervousness takes hold. It's an exciting feeling; the feeling of new beginning and an end to confusion and loneliness. We took a long road to finally find a place called home. I'm grateful for the journey. By his side, from now until forever, is where I belong.

"Dui... you're too... experienced... for a virgin."

Gentle hands have crawled to all the right places, burning lips set my spirit on fire, and those arms hold me just right that I feel indescribably loved and desired. The touch of his fingers on my bare skin is so exhilarating, all discretion have flown out the window. Crying out his name doesn't relieve this aching torment inside. I wish to feel more of him, yet barely have I parted his shirt, Dui's lips descend my bare chest, diverging at my heart for one of the heaving mounds. His free hand grasps the other.

"I've dreamt of loving you this way so many nights and felt the ache of reality by day. If this is another dream, don't wake me. Let me love you for the thousandth time."

That confession is strangely lewd and romantic. The truth is I've thought about him too. By all means, he has been patient and meticulous in making our first night together everything I'd hope and more. I'm on the verge of losing my mind. Dui must merely give into his own pleasure for my fantasy to fully realize.

Swallowing the cry that rises on impulse, my final desirous request flows into his ear in a breathless whisper. Though startled from hearing the lurid pleas for the first time, Dui doesn't hesitate in affirming the reality of our affair through an act so vivid and intense that dreams can never imitate. A kiss seals our promise of eternity just as we become one. Indescribable rising sensations of love and lust leave me utterly speechless. I would scream my love for him if I still had my voice.

My heart, my body, my soul. Every bit of me has melded to Dui. I am no longer mine and he is no longer his. We belong to each other, losing our sense of self in a most wondrous mean. Even then, even when I can't tell heads from tails, can't do else but desperately cling to Dui, my lover continues pouring his love until I'm drowning beneath the waves.

As the dark of night slowly creeps into the room from the shrouded moon, the world around feels surreal. We've reached a blissful infinity where time seemingly stands still. In my arms is Dui and in Dui's arms is me. Nothing else matters. His hazy grey eyes reflect the sentiment dominating mine.

"I love you," he whispers again for the hundredth time.

Unable to fend off what comes next, he smiles a tender smile to express every word that can't be formed in the clouded satisfaction which overtakes every lover's first night. The first time is most strenuous. I'm happy his first time was with me.

"And I love you," is the muffled return from his chest where I've buried my face. He smells of dried herbs, the scent of home. "Thank you for loving me, Dui."

"The pleasure's all mine, love."

Peaceful slumber comes to lull away consciousness. Our arms bind one another tightly so that we would not part, even in our dreams. Dui strokes my head gently, his hand slows with every touch from rising fatigue.

Those many years ago, a quiet boy walked into Tian Mao Yi. A brutish, cross-dressed girl couldn't help but tormented him. At the time, unspoken rivalry set them apart. Though, now that I look back, Hu was right. I pestered Dui because I liked him. I wanted his attention. I wanted to provoke passion from disinterested grey eyes. For a time, life took us in different paths and fate eventually brought us back. From the first moment we met, my heart stirred as if beating for the first time. This time and into eternity, my heart will beat solely for Dui.

As the two worlds begin to blur, a distant whisper of love gives sweet reminder of the adventures in life still waiting to be experienced. Together, each moment will be more beautiful than the last.

The End.

www.ingramcontent.com/pod-product-compliance
Lightning Source LLC
Chambersburg PA
CBHW062129170626
46813CB00002B/623